JESSICA

*She's beautiful,
smart ... and
heartbroken*

D. N. WATTS

JESSICA

First Edition, May, 2021

Copyright © 2021 Debby-Ann Watts

Written by D. N. Watts

Contact Info: ephiphany.debby@gmail.com

D. N. WATTS

*To my family, just
skip the sex scenes*

1

Staring at herself in the mirror, Jessica Clarke was mesmerized by her beauty. Her bright sultry brown eyes and glowing dark chocolate skin were intensified when a sudden sliver of sunlight streaked through the curtains hung at her bedroom window. Thank you mummy! She thought.

Her alarm sounded, startling her back to reality. She had a ton of errands to run today and she needed to get to it. Brushing her gelled hair into a high bun, she began searching for a scrunchie to hold her thick curly mane in place.

"Oh jeez, my arm is hurting, where the hell is it," she sighed in aggravation as she dug through all the crap in her vanity drawers searching.

"Damn, hear it is!" With two quick twists and turns of her wrist, her hair was in place and she finished up by slicking her baby hair in place. Now she was ready.

Jessica was meeting her oldest sister Charmaine for a quick bite to eat and to catch up with her. She also wanted to tell her about her exciting news. Charmaine was barely five years older than Jessica and coming from a family of five sisters, all top achievers, Jessica was very happy to share her impressive news.

Hitting the road, she went to one of the popular malls twenty minutes from her home, to spend money she had no business spending. She had her eyebrows threaded, collected packages from her post office box and deposited three cheques to her bank account. She paid her bills and was now heading to lunch with her sissy. Jessica and Charmaine had the closest relationship out of their siblings.

Being the middle child was not easy for Jessica. She felt that she was always overlooked and was taunted by her sisters and therefore left to her own devices. She recalled that when she was younger, while playing with her mother's makeup, she accidently broke a very expensive face cream, which her mother prided as the key to her youthful glow. She started to tremble in fear, thinking of the horrible beating she was sure to endure when her mother found out. Charmaine saw that her sister was on the verge of a nervous breakdown, so she took the fall for her and told their mother that it was broke with her by accident. This initially forged the incredible bond between big sister and little sister.

Growing up, Charmaine took Jessica under her wing. She spoke to her about boys and puberty and she gave her little articles to read about what to expect during puberty and the female genitalia. She even gave her financial advice before she even entered high school; it was never too early to learn about saving your coins. Jessica trusted her sister completely and it was Charmaine whom she confided in when she became a woman and experienced her first menstrual cycle; her first crush and her first 'time'. They knew each other's secrets and always kept it real with each other even when it was going to hurt.

Whilst driving on her way to lunch, she glanced at her nails, wrapped around the steering wheel. Jessica was disgusted at how shabby her nails looked and could only imagine what the hell her toes looked like since her nails looked like shit. But, at least her hair was cute,

"Yessss!" she whispered beneath her breath as she peeped her cute reflection in the rearview mirror.

Jessica totally enjoyed viewing the scenery and architecture of the homes she passed as she drove through the country side, making her way to the restaurant which was located outside of the hustle and bustle of the city. "Ohhh, this is my song"... she turned the volume up high on the car stereo. "...love you to the end of time..." Jessica sang her best sultry Mariah Carey impersonation, along with the lip quivering while using her free hand as a pretend microphone, she didn't care who saw her.

"Finally," she breathed, she made it to the restaurant and exited her car into the midday heat. The intense heat hit her like hell on earth. "Got damn, it's hot as hell today, gosh."

Not one for the sun, Jessica made her way quickly inside. She spotted her sister immediately sitting in the back on her phone. She greeted the hostess, simultaneously pointing her sister out to him and sashayed over, to the annoyance of Charmaine.

"Why you always gotta be so extra bitch?" Charmaine said dryly, eyeing Jessica up and down.

"Girrlllll bye," flinging her "talk to the hand" gesture in Charmaine's face. "Why you always gotta be on yo' phone then Charmaine." After a few seconds of silence, they both busted out laughing.

"Actually, I was informing *our* parents that I was waiting on you to meet me for lunch, mum said she has not heard from you in a few days, what's up with that?"

Rolling her eyes Jessica, sighed, "I've been busy, ok!"

Jessica inwardly scolded herself and promised to call her mum and dad as soon as possible.

"So! What's up with you and Ron?"

"Damn, can a bitch eat before you get all up in her business, not a how are you?...not a how was your day?, nothing!" Jessica said sucking her teeth, she was beyond annoyed. "We aight," she said straight faced.

"What does that mean boo?"

"It means we aight!" Jessica was getting increasingly annoyed by the second and was not about to let her sister spoil her moment with stupid questions.

Before Charmaine could go on further, Jessica continued, "Anyway, I've scored a big ass town home and I have a buyer.

It's been three years since Jessica received her Real Estate Licence from Conwell College. Super excited and ready to make some coin, she interned at numerous real estate companies, soaking up as much knowledge as she could from those around her. Being in a competitive field like hers and with a collapsing economy to boot, business was slow to non-existent, but if anyone knew Jessica, knew she never gave up.

In any event, her family wasn't filthy rich but they certainly weren't poor either, if she needed anything, they were happy and willing to help.

Finally catching a break in summer of 2009, Jessica co-broke a three storey mansion deep in the suburbs for $1,500,000.00, the commission on that was pretty sweet and to celebrate, she bought herself a sweet little ride, the car of her dreams. Her introduction to the movers and shakers of society was exciting and was her driving force to success. Building her portfolio was an impressive feat that sometimes frightened and intrigued her at the same time.

Excitedly, she began spilling the details of the new property which she advertised for sale a few days ago.

"I posted this recently," smacking a colourful glossy flyer on the table, it showcased a gorgeous five bedroom, four bathroom luxury home on 5 acres of land on the outskirts of the city, with amazing views of the coastline going for two million dollars.

"Ohhhhhh, this is gorgeous, do you have any viable prospects?" Charmaine asked intrigued.

"I just told you I have a buyer. Charmaine, pay attention. Anyway since you asked, pass this flyer around at your office in case this potential buyer pulls out, test the pond really, see if anyone of your clients would be interested or know of someone who would be interested in this beauty."

Charmaine owned her very own dental practice that catered to an elite clientele. Jessica prayed that her sister could bring her potential clients.

"Fine, I'll spring it to a few people and let you know. So, back to you and Ron!"

"Girl, you and this Ron, Ron, Ron, oh my gosh! How are you and Jeffrey?" Jessica countered. Jeffrey was Charmaine's husband of eight years and also her business partner.

"Better yet, give it to Jeffrey too, his golfing buddies could be useful," she said coyly.

"Well?"

Jessica sighed loudly.

As she thought back to her last conversation with Ron two weeks prior, her eyes became misty. A reaction, that did not go unnoticed by Charmaine.

"What's wrong sis?" Charmaine asked cautiously, simultaneously preparing herself to hear some type of tragic news.

"He's...uhhh....going back to his wife and kids.

2

A tickly sensation alerted Jessica that tears were running down her cheeks. Grabbing a tissue from the holder on the table, she dabbed her tears and looked sadly at her sister who was sitting across from her, obviously dumbfounded.

She remembered that it was the week before Christmas, 2013. She was invited to a Christmas dinner/party at one of her friend's homes. There she was, 27 years old, dressed to the nines in a body hugging cold shoulder white mini dress, black heels, body on 10, chilling and chatting, being social and having a fantastic time. Jessica knew that she looked fire and was going to show every curve she owned that night.

Jessica from a very young age, was always told by family and peers that she was a beautiful girl. It took her years to appreciate that sentiment. She was so accustomed to stares from men and women that it no longer phased her. Whether it was going grocery shopping, showing properties or just walking outside she was constantly propositioned.

Being beautiful according to her, had its ups and downs. She never took herself too seriously and knew that a hot body was not all she needed to make it in the world. She needed brains too.

"Do you believe in love at first sight, or should I walk by again." A voice came from next to her.

Jessica swiveled her neck to see who the hell was disturbing her zen with some lame ass line. She was ready to send him on his way with a few choice words. Turning, she gazed into the prettiest hazel eyes she'd ever seen on a man in all her life.

All sass escaped her and she melted like butter. "I've never heard that one before, where did you get that line from, your homeboys?" she asked feigning annoyance.

Laughing, he said, "No, I read it somewhere," he extended his hand for a handshake and she shook it, a tad bit too long if she would admit it to herself. "I am Ron Bishop, Ronald Bishop," he said smiling, "It's very nice to meet you. I noticed you when you arrived and I thought I'd introduce myself."

"My pleasure, I'm Jessica Clarke," Jessica could not believe this tall, well built, fine ass man was in her presence. She was immediately in lust. She suddenly realized, they were still holding hands, she slowly and very regrettably released his hand. Wickedly, she slid her fingers through his palm. A shiver of excitement ran down her spine.

Touching his chiseled arms was almost electric. His honey coloured skin was smooth and rich, the contrast of his dark beard gave him an almost seductive appearance. Ohhh yesss, Jessica was in lust, she wanted to rub her hands all over his broad chest. He seemed well off too. She peeped his expensive watch, tailored black slacks and polished shiny black shoes. Ron was 40 years old, a successful Investment Banker and better yet, very, very attractive. For Jessica, *age ain't nothing but a number.*

"What the hell do you mean he's going back to his wife?" Charmaine asked incredulously, practically shouting the words and staring bugged eyed at her sister. If the atmosphere at the table wasn't so tense, she would have had a good laugh at her sister's bug eyed appearance. Thankfully, the restaurant was not full and no one observed the interaction happening at their table.

"Lower your got damn voice one, and two, I said he's rekindling with his wife, the mother of his children," sighing, she took a big gulp of wine, trying not to choke on the words that just left her mouth.

Just then the waiter approached their table and took their drinks and food orders. Within seconds, the waiter returned with two glasses of red wine.

Grateful for the distraction, Jessica adjusted her blouse and twirled the tear-filled tissue in her hand, avoiding the glare of her older sibling who was waiting with bated breath.

Once the waiter was out of ear shot, Jessica mumbled, "It is what it is!"

"Girl that's bullshit and you know it," Charmaine was clearly annoyed.

"I really don't want to get into this right now, but, he said it's something he feels he has to do for his kids." Jessica went silent for a few minutes, lost in her thoughts.

For two months Ron and Jessica dated heavily, things got hot and heavy super fast and soon she was head over heels in love with him. Trips, vacations together, shopping, wherever you saw Ron, you saw Jessica and vice versa. Even though Ron was much older, he didn't lack in the bedroom, which was a huge surprise to Jessica. She was not expecting him to be so voracious, but he was and she also loved that he was a cuddler and that made him so much more sexy to her.

Jessica heard Charmaine repeatedly calling her name and refocused her attention to her sister. The waiter had returned and was placing their orders on the table.

"Where did you go just now? I am so sorry this is happening to you. How are you handling all this?" Charmaine asked as the waiter disappeared in the back section of the restaurant.

Releasing a long breath, Jessica bowed her head and started to sob over her braised lamb chops and creamed green beans.

Charmaine took her sister's hand in hers and prayed a silent prayer.

With the strained look on Jessica's face, Charmaine decided not to press her sister for further details, she decided to wait until Jessica was good and ready to talk.

They ate in silence for the rest of the meal.

They sat for another hour, chatting idly of current news in the newspapers and of family until they'd eaten their fill.

Jessica paid for lunch even though it was her sister who invited her to lunch. As they gathered their purses to prepare to leave, her cell rang, singing her favourite Biggie Irie soca tune. Her eyes quickly read the display screen of the call, she turned the screen to her sister so she could see the caller's name. It was Ron.

She answered, her voice sounding more upbeat than she actually felt.

"Hi!" she said, "What's up?"

"Uhhh, I wanted to talk with you. I was calling you at home but there was no answer. Are you at home?"

"No. I'll be there in a few, I'll shout you then," She ended the call.

Things were definitely different between them, you could hear the underlying sadness in both their voices. Jessica knew that Ron loved her and she him, but it just wasn't meant to be.

"What does he want now?" Charmaine asked as Jessica put her phone away.

"Let's go outside." Walking towards the exit of the restaurant, Jessica felt incredibly sad. Hearing Ron's voice really made her yearn to be with him at that exact moment. "He just wants to talk," she said almost to herself.

"Talk about what?" she said with her hand akimbo. "You shouldn't even have taken his call, matter of fact, block his ass and delete his number while you're at it, the nerve of his trifling ass."

Trying not to get into a heated argument with her sis, she walked to her car with Charmaine still cussing and fussing behind her. She unlocked her door and flung her bag across the front seat and wished her sister a safe trip home.

Before she could close her door all the way shut, she barely heard her sis asking "What are you gonna tell mom and dad?" Charmaine asked.

With that Jessica started her car and flew out of the car park to avoid having to answer her sister. The thought of breaking the news of another failed relationship was more terrifying than Charmaine could ever understand.

3

Jessica sat on her couch in her living room feeling miserable, should she call him or not. She nibbled at her nails whilst debating what to do. Bursting from her seat, she opted for a warm bath and a good movie to drown the thoughts from her head.

Dressed in her terry cloth robe, she searched her tv guide for something interesting to watch. Propping pillows behind her back she noticed her work chart on the coffee table, picking it up she thought she could get in a little work while she watched tv.

As she sat there flipping through her chart and making notes, her cell chirped indicating that she had received a message. It was Charmaine scolding her about leaving her standing in the parking lot and querying if she reached home safely. She replied quickly with an apology and settled back down to continue working and watching tv.

Her phone chirped again. Thinking it was her sister again, she ignored it.

Again her cell chirped. Irritated, she yanked it up from the couch and looked at the display. It was Ron.

Tears settled in her eyes once more. She wondered where in the hell did they go wrong.

Flashing back to their first official date, Jessica recalled how Ron took her on a double date with another couple. They were a lovely couple who gave Jessica a little personal insight into Ron. He played college ball, was a star athlete, incredibly business savy and was an overall gentleman. Jessica was sold completely on Ron. The way her face lit up when she looked at him; the way he looked at her in return, people could tell instantly that they were in deeply in love.

After five months of dating, it was time to introduce her parents to her future husband and she was very excited.

It was on her parents' 50th Wedding Anniversary dinner, that she introduced Ron to her parents, Mr. Stephen Clarke and Mrs. Sabrina Clarke and her immediate family. The dinner was amazing. The outpouring of love and glowing sentiments expressed to her parents through song and poems made it a night to remember. Jessica's parents were thoroughly impressed with Ron. He was tall and handsome, intellectual and humorous. "I like him," her mother quipped in her ear. Mr, Clarke, however, was not so easily won over, just like a father, he cautioned Ron about breaking his daughter's heart.

Jessica prayed that she would have that same deep love and connection similar to her parents whenever she got married.

One year later, Jessica and Ron moved in together in her home.

Life was sweet and business was booming. Jessica even helped Ron with a few investment opportunities to increase his real estate portfolio.

"How do you feel about us getting married?" she asked while playing with his curly black hair. Ron was laying in the bed with his head on resting in her lap.

"Are you ready for marriage?" she asked, "We've been together for awhile."

"I'm not sure," he said.

Speaking of which, "I have yet to meet your folks," she persisted.

"It's not on purpose hunny, I'll make sure you meet them soon." He got on his knees and pulled her under him, he kissed her exposed stomach, trailing light kisses all the way down her navel, he then pulled her silk panties off with his teeth and began tasting her, slipping his tongue inside of her softness, Jessica writhed and bucked her hips against his sweet tongue, she sunk her hand into his hair, working her hips in a circular motion against his stiff tongue until she climaxed.

Ron licked his lips and laid next to Jessica as her shivers subsided. He kissed her slowly and deliberately.

Ron wiped his mouth with the back of his hand and Jessica settled back against her bed.

"Are you hungry?" he asked.

Jessica moaned. Her body was still in recovery mode.

"Ok then," he playfully slapped her on her thigh and headed downstairs to the kitchen.

With Ron making lunch, Jessica took a quick shower and later joined him in the kitchen.

"I know what you just did there," her tone serious.

"Whattttt?" he started laughing.

"Sir. That's not gonna work over here. Are you scared to get married?" she prodded.

Ron went silent.

"It's not that at all," He said.

"Then what is it?" she continued.

"When the time is right, it'll happen," he stated.

"You should know by now, if you want to get married to me or not," she persisted.

"I do baby," he said, tossing the Caesar salad and avoiding all eye contact with her.

"I'm serious. If you don't want to get married, we should end this now." Jessica was pissed.

Jessica stormed out onto the patio and slammed the door.

Ron wiped his hands in a kitchen towel and went onto the patio to join her.

"It's not that I don't want to marry you Jess. I have some things that I need to deal with before I can make that commitment to you, that's all," His voice was stern.

Jessica turned and faced him.

"Ok so how long before you deal with whatever you have to deal with?" she asked.

"I don't know," he said looking directly at her.

Jessica frowned.

"So I'm just supposed to continue fucking you and living with you until infinity? Man, fuck this shit!" She got up and pushed past him. She flopped onto the couch and flipped on the tv. She was not in a tv mood but she needed a distraction.

Ron stayed on the patio, thinking. He loved Jessica, he just couldn't marry her right now. He rubbed his eyes and clasp his hands beneath his chin, praying. Jessica couldn't concentrate on the tv, she grabbed her keys and purse and headed outside. She sat in her car, thinking on where to go. Just drive, she thought.

She took off, turning her radio up high, she thought of her conversation with Ron. She knew that his trying to please her sexually was another stall tactic to stop her from the marriage conversation. She was tired of him beating around the bush. He either wanted her or not, it was really that simple in her opinion.

She stopped at a fast food joint north of Wilkinson Road and grabbed a chicken salad and sprite; she parked and ate before returning home.

"You could have at least said you were leaving," he said when she stepped through the door.

Jessica was still irritated. Irritated by the fact that this man, that was living in her home, did not want to marry her.

"I needed to be alone," she replied.

"I left your dinner in the oven," he was watching her intently.

"I'm not hungry," she looked at him coldly.

She tossed her keys on the hallway table and flew up the stairs, she did not want to look at him, she felt emotional and stressed.

She turned on the tv in her bedroom and found an interesting documentary on the artic seals, she loved the National Geographic channel and their programmes on wildlife and nature.

Ron came into the bedroom and sat on the end of the bed and faced her.

"I love you. You know that," he said solemnly.

She didn't respond.

Jessica hardly spoke to Ron for the rest of the evening, he spent most of his time downstairs, on the living room couch on his laptop. He was monitoring the stock market and creating reports for his vast clientele.

At 9:00 p.m. Ron came up, showered and got into bed, he turned away from Jessica and soon he was asleep. Jessica stared at his back, the rise and fall of his back indicated he was sound asleep. She made up in her mind that if a proposal did not happen by summer, she was out.

4

As they prepared for work the next day, Jessica informed Ron that she was going to be home late that day.

"Ok. Why?" he asked.

"Uhh, I have a showing at 6:00 p.m. over on Park Way Avenue," she offered.

Ron was dressed in his usual tailored work suit. She loved having a corporate man. He was always well dressed and his beard and hair remained groomed to perfection.

She loved him, she could not deny that.

She was dressed in a simple white dress, it fit her figure perfectly. She walked past him and he stopped her in her tracks, he took her hand and pulled her into him. He kissed her hungrily. She tried to push him off but he was too strong, she honestly couldn't resist him either, he stood her against the kitchen wall and lifted her off the floor, pressing his hardness into her and she instinctively wrapped her legs around him.

Frenzied, he freed his manhood from his pants and hiked her dress up, he ripped her panties off and slammed his swollen shaft deep inside of her. A swish of air escaped Jessica lips. As he pumped in and out of her, the hate and anger she felt towards him disappeared, she climaxed, squeezing his manhood with her walls as she flexed her hips up and down. Ron growled as he came, he withdrew from her and released his seed on her thigh. He eased her legs down and she re-arranged her dress and took her torn undies from the floor. They made eye contact but said nothing to each other.

"I need to shower," she said.

"Me too," he was looking for evidence that they were ok.

Jessica eased past him, heading to her bedroom, she stripped and entered the shower.

Ron entered seconds later.

They made love once more in the shower. He stroked her back "I love you." He finally said.

"I love you too," she replied.

They toweled off and dressed again. Jessica reapplied her makeup, fixed her hair and tossed their previous clothing into the laundry basket.

They headed downstairs and grabbed their lunches. Jessica hooked her purse on her shoulder and they set off to work. That Monday when Jessica returned home from work, Ron had cooked them a lovely meal and she was pleasantly surprised.

There was fried chicken, fried cabbage, orange rice and red wine chilling in the cooler.

"You cooked?" she asked when he came over and

kissed her.

"I did. I'm waving the white flag," he winked.

"Hmm, I'mma go shower and come back."

Jessica returned fifteen minutes later dressed in a loosely fitted T-shirt.

"Sit mi lady," Ron stated in a horrible fake Irish accent.

"Thank you," she said.

"How was your day?" she asked, serving herself a little bit of everything.

"Rough. I think I need a vacation," she said dryly.

"Me too but I can't right now, too much going on at work," she said.

"We definitely need to go somewhere this summer," he continued.

"We'll see how it goes," she said chewing slowly.

"Fine," he took a sip of his red wine.

Jessica opted for a beer. She was trying to ignore the gnawing feeling creeping up her spine, she was not sure how long she could wait on Ron to pop the question.

After dinner, they piled the dirty dishes into the dishwasher and took seats in living room; they switched the tv on and huddled together on the couch catching a few shows. Eventually they went to bed around 10:00 p.m. and had sex for the third time that day. Ron was insatiable and he couldn't get enough of Jessica, she didn't mind the sex, however, she strongly believed that she needed more than just a roll in the hay.

She made another lunch date with Charmaine for later that day at Ned's Bistro, a lunch spot across from her workplace, she needed to talk to someone.

Jessica pulled up to a gorgeous two story home, huge bay windows sat on the first story and a walkout deck on the second story. An enclosed pool sat on the eastern side of the property.

Jessica was there to meet three potential buyers and

she was scheduled to be there awhile. Her first potential buyer pulled up and Jessica exited her car to greet him, single male, no kids; he constantly hit on Jessica, she smiled and tolerated him, he wasn't interested in the house at all; a waste of her time. The second potential buyers were a young couple, no kids as yet, but they were interested in raising a family in the area and work was only thirty minutes away; most definitely two viable prospects. The third potential buyers were a middle aged couple with adult children and two grandchildren, they were looking for a family home to accommodate everyone and fell in love with the property, they were adamant in securing this home. Jessica promised to draw up the paperwork for them to submit to their mortgage lender.

Before leaving for lunch, Jessica informed her boss that she would not be returning to work.

"Ok! See you tomorrow," he said, not looking up from his paperwork.

Jessica packed her bag and slung her purse over her shoulder, she left her building and jaywalked over to the Bistro, she was seated and she ordered a glass of white wine while she waited.

Charmaine arrived soon after. "Hey, what's so important that you couldn't talk over the phone?" she said as she sat. Charmaine was dressed in a cute purple skirt and pink loose blouse.

"Cute fit," Jessica said sipping on her drink.

"Remember how I told you I've been asking Ron about marriage?" she began.

"Yeah, he's hesitant for some reason," she replied.

"Well, we were talking the other day and I brought it up to him again and he still can't or won't give me a straight answer," she said angrily.

"He has to be hiding something," Charmaine

mused.

"Like what?" she piped up.

"I'm not sure," she said.

"He said that uhhh he has things to tidy up first."

"That's bullshit. What got damn things?" Charmaine shrieked.

Jessica shrugged.

"If he doesn't propose by April; I'm done."

"That's easier said than done, sissy," she said sullenly.

Jessica leaned in. "Is it wrong to want more? I'm giving all of me for what? Yes, I love the gifts and the trips, but..." Jessica said teary eyed, "Almost two years and you're still unsure?"

"Hmmm."

"I think you should speak to him one more time and if he's still hesitant, then cut your losses."

"Arghhhh. This is so aggravating. I could have any man I want and I'm saying to him it's you I want, yet I'm being strung along."

"I understand. I would feel the same way." Charmaine added.

"We live together, like what's the problem? I don't want to resent him but I will if I stay in this relationship."

"Jess, you need to let him know how you feel," she said soothingly.

"I already did that!" she shouted. "I'm sorry. I didn't mean to yell at you," Jessica said.

"It's cool."

"I gotta go," Jessica said.

"Bitch, you asked me here and now you wanna go. I haven't even eaten yet." Charmaine blurted out.

"Damn. Order your fricking food and let me go," she said smugly.

Charmaine signaled the waiter and placed her

order. Jessica ordered a meal for later.

They chatted for another hour, giving Charmaine enough time to eat and digest her meal.

Finally, Jessica was headed home.

She reflected on her conversation with her sister as she drove. She decided to have a final chat with Ron...soon.

Little did she know, life was about to throw Jessica a huge curveball.

5

Jessica prepared a small salad for dinner, she heated the left over chicken from their previous dinner the night before, she plated Ron's and took it to him in the office just off of the living room.

After dinner, Ron was upset and agitated.

"What's wrong? You're acting really weird tonight," Jessica queried.

She leaned into him, cupping his face in her hands. They shared a long passionate kiss until he abruptly pulled away. He straightened up on the living room couch and cleared his throat before he began to speak.

"I have something to tell you." He took a slow long breath.

"What is it?" she was scared he was about to tell her he was dying. Her heart was racing.

"I don't know how to say this except to just say it.

I'm married," he stared at her, waiting for some type of confirmation that she heard what he said.

"I am married, Jessica" he repeated. "Well separated. My wife and I are separated. For the last two years. We've been separated...for the last two years," he rattled on.

Jessica subconsciously pinched her ears; she could hardly believe what she was hearing.

"And!" he looked defeated, "We have two children together, a boy and girl. They are six and eight years old," he breathed deeply before looking away.

"What do you mean you're married?" she asked. Confusion and anger flashed across her face. "Married to who? Wait. How can you be married? We've been together for almost 2 years?"

"Baby..., we were separated before you and I met."

"You've never ever mentioned having any kids," she said confused.

Jessica could hardly believe what she was hearing. The man she loved, wanted to marry and have a family with was sitting on her couch, in her home telling her that he was married!

"I'm sorry baby, I knew that I should have told you sooner. I was so scared I'd lose you, please I'm so sorry."

"Get the fuck out!" she screamed, "Get out now!"

"Jess..."

"Getttt Outttt!" she screamed again, uncontrollable rage radiating through her body, tears rushed from her eyes like rain water gushing from a drain after a storm.

"Jessica we have to talk this through," He insisted.

"GET OUT!" Jessica screamed.

"AND GO WHERE?" he shouted back.

"I don't give a fuck," she was hysterical.

Jessica burst into the guest bathroom and slammed

the door shut.

"FUCK," she heard Ron yell as she slammed the door.

Ron grabbed his keys and jacket and seconds later was peeling away in his car. Jessica could hear the tires screeching as he pulled away from the curb.

Once she was sure he was gone, she locked her front door and slid the chain in place. She staggered into the living room, crumpling to the floor beside her couch. Jessica could hardly breathe, peering through her tears she pulled her throw from the couch to muffle her heart wrenching cries. Pulling her knees up to her chest, she laid there trying to catch her breath. Jessica stayed in that position until the wee hours of the morning, silent tears still leaking from her eyes.

As the sun rose in the distance, the once dark living room came alive with the sounds of daybreak. The birds were chirping and she could hear the early morning traffic outside.

Jessica took a deep breath and heaved herself from the floor to the couch. There she replayed the events of last night in her head. How could he do that to her, just calmly reveal to her he's married or separated. Whatever the hell that meant. A searing pain shot through her head and she eased her back onto the couch and tried to control her rapid heartbeat.

Checking the clock sitting on top of her fireplace, she saw it was soon time for her to start preparing for work. Sluggishly, she dragged herself to her bedroom to shower and dress. She sat at her vanity, still in her damp towel and studied her reflection in the mirror, huge bags had formed beneath her eyes and she looked haggard and sleepy. "Shit, I need some coffee, stat," she said.

Jessica styled her hair as best she could and applied makeup to hide the dark circles under her eyes. When she was confident that she looked presentable at least, she quickly made a cup of coffee, grabbed her purse, her work bag and laptop and left for work.

Placing everything in the back of her car, she closed the door and slid into the driver's seat and pulled out into traffic. Her heart was breaking and she had no idea how to put the pieces back together. Fresh tears ran freely down her cheeks, it was difficult for her to see the road. She was blinking incessantly to clear the water from her eyes similar to wipers on a car. She considered reporting ill to work and returning home and flying straight in the bed. She had no desire to work but knew she had to keep her mind busy. She didn't want to relive the terror of last night.

After three showings to prospective buyers, Jessica returned to the office, there, she updated a few reports, attended a corporate meeting and returned several calls to clients. As the work day ended, she gathered her purse, work bag, laptop and cell and headed to the car park.

Once on the road, her stomach growled reminding her she hadn't eaten all day. She diverted to one of her favourite drive-through fast food restaurants and ordered some comfort food and was back on the road within five minutes.

Dropping her keys, bag and purse on her black granite kitchen countertop, she searched her refridgerator for something sweet to drink, finding nothing she took a bottle of water. She set up her dinner in front of the tv. She wanted to relax and enjoy her meal all the while forcing herself not to reflect on the terror she was subjected to last night. Deep down she knew it was over. She was mortified of what this failed relationship really meant for her future plans.

The next day Jessica got up, did her usual routine

and headed to work. She had not heard Ron and even though she really didn't want to talk to him it bothered her deeply that he was not at her door begging her forgiveness. Jessica made the immediate decision not to tell her sister Charmaine the events of that night until she was sure of what she was going to do.

One week later, Jessica pulled into her driveway, she noticed a car similar to Ron's car parked on the curb outside of her home. She peeped through her rearview mirror; it was definitely him waiting for her to return home from work. This she was not prepared for plus she was not in the mood to argue but she did have questions and he was the only person that could answer them.

Still she was not ready.

Jessica approached the car and knocked hard on the window.

Ron was startled; he turned off his ignition, opened his car door and stepped out.

Tension passed between them and no one wanted to speak first.

Seeing Ron face to face, unable to touch him or kiss him made Jessica's heart burn in agony. She honestly did love this man.

"Hi, can we go inside?" Ron asked cautiously, trying to gauge her reaction.

"No. I'm really tired, why are you here?" Jessica said sharply.

"We need to talk...I..."

Jessica abruptly turned and walked away not letting Ron finish his sentence.

"Jessica! Please. Just let me explain!" Ron shrieked.

"Jessica!" he called again.

Jessica was at her door; she unlocked it and stepped inside, leaving Ron behind calling her name.

Closing the door behind her, Jessica ran to her

window. Ron was back in his car. She heard him start his car engine and saw him driving away.

Suddenly, all the hurt, pain and anger she felt a few days ago came rushing back and she felt helpless to control the loud sobs that were escaping her. Sobs so intense, that her stomach muscles contracted as she heaved with each sob.

Twenty minutes later the sobs subsided, Jessica found herself bent at her kitchen sink splashing cold water on her face. She stood upright, pulled open her refridgerator and grabbed the first bottle of wine she saw.

Plucking a wine glass from her cabinet above the sink, she headed to her bedroom patio. She sat, deep in thought while sipping her wine. Jessica stayed there until she felt the chill of the night setting in.

Since tomorrow was Saturday, she decided to down the last bit of wine remaining in the bottle. Tucking the empty wine bottle beneath one arm and clasping the empty glass in her free hand, she made her way inside of her bedroom. Plopping on the bed, she realized that she was still in her work attire. She was too achy to move and she eventually fell asleep with fresh tears soaking into her pillow.

Jessica felt searing heat on the back of her legs. Straining her neck to see what was burning her so terribly, she realized she was face down on her bed and the sun was beaming through her window directly unto her. Rolling over on her back Jessica struggled slightly to sit upright.

Feeling lightheaded, she crashed back onto the bed and stared at her ceiling, praying to God for strength to overcome her torment and heal her broken heart. Closing her eyes, she slipped back to sleep for another hour.

Her eyes flew open, she could hear her cell ringing in the distance.

Rolling off the bed, she went in search of her cell, barely seeing the caller ID through her sleepy eyes, she quickly answered on the last ring.

It was Charmaine.

"Hey sis, I haven't heard you all week, everything okay?"

"Yea, I've been super busy with work etc," she lied.

After exchanging pleasantries, Jessica soon wrapped up the call and headed to the kitchen to cook breakfast.

Not sure what she felt like eating, she finally chose something simple; eggs, toast and coffee. Ron's favourite. How ironic. After breakfast, Jessica returned to her patio and called her parents. She repeated the same pleasantries as she did with Charmaine, apologized for being tardy in calling and promised to call them sometime next week.

6

Since it was the weekend, Jessica did laundry, sanitized and cleaned her home and then sat in her office to focus on her work, dedicating two hours to reports and responding emails from clients and her boss. When night finally set in Jessica decided to journal, it was not something she did regularly, but when she felt the need to vent, outside of humans, she preferred to write everything down. Pouring her heart out in her journal, she expressed her hurt, fears and mental and emotional burdens. After rereading what she scribed she closed her diary and closed her eyes.

Jessica allowed herself to stew in her emotions, she felt to cry but didn't. She needed to regain control and the only way to do this was to speak to Ron.

As her thoughts drifted back to the present, she somberly recalled, it was two weeks ago since Ron was parked outside of her home trying to engage her.

Reluctantly, she took her cell out and slowly punched in Ron's number.

"Thanks for calling me back," he said.

"What did you want?" she asked frowning.

"Can I come over, to talk?" he asked sorrowfully.

Audibly sighing, she said "Ok. Be here in 15 minutes." Jessica hung up and set the phone down. Was she doing the right thing? Should she just cut him off? Numerous questions were rushing through her mind making her increasingly anxious.

Finally she went to her room, showered and got comfy in her fluffy pajamas top and long pants. The doorbell rang and she walked to the door and cautiously spied through the peephole. It was Ron.

Jessica took a long, deep, calming breath before opening the door. There he stood. Her Adonis, her lying ass Adonis. Jessica rolled her eyes as Ron entered and walked past her headed for the living room. He sat on the couch and waited for her to sit next to him.

Glancing at the clock it was 7:20 p.m. This was going to be a long ass evening.

Jessica really wanted to get a glass of wine to calm her nerves but thought better of it and made her way to the couch opposite Ron.

As soon as she sat, Ron rubbed both his palms over his entire face and began his diatribe.

"I never meant to hurt you baby," he began.

"Why didn't you tell me once we started being serious with each other?" she asked cutting straight to the chase.

"I wanted to. The time never seemed right. My biggest regret would be not being honest with you from the start," Looking directly into her eyes, he continued.

"The reason I was not giving you a solid answer about marriage was because I didn't know how to fix my life, meaning my relationship with my ex....I've been struggling with so much pain. I feel as though I'm hurting my kids by not being there full time. They keep asking when I'm returning home." His face contorted as he recalled those memories, "It kills my soul every time," he continued.

"Hhmmm" Jessica mumbled. Jessica wrapped both her arms tightly around her body, trying to keep her composure.

"I miss them so much," he said as tears freely flowed from his eyes. Wiping at his eyes with his hand he paused, adjusting himself in his seat.

"I don't understand, what's stopping you from having a relationship with your kids?" she queried.

Ron began to explain that after his kids were born, his marriage started to suffer. His marriage eventually became strained, due to his demanding career and schedule. He was never home and regrettably missed numerous milestones in his kids' young lives. It all came to a head, when his wife asked him to move out two years ago.

He noticed his kids would no longer eagerly greet him at the door when he came to visit. They were not happy with the toys and gifts he would bring them for Christmas, birthdays or just because. As they grew older they seemed sad and withdrawn whenever he was around.

His decision to return to his wife was not an easy one, but one he felt there was no other choice.

"I really have no idea what to do. That night when we first met I was hesitant to introduce myself. Your energy was so captivating that I had to find out more about you. I do love you Jessica, never ever doubt that," he said reassuringly.

Tears welled in both of their eyes. Longing and need enveloped them. Swiftly Ron approached her on the couch and quickly lifted her up in his arms and kissed her passionately. Though she resisted, her body screamed for his touch. Jessica leaned into his chest as he carried her to her bedroom. She truly loved waking up in Ron's arms, her legs were normally slung across his thighs, she would often listen to his light snore and breathing. This morning, however, was different.

Looking up at the ceiling, with her arm propped behind her head, Jessica repositioned Ron's arm off of her. It became clear to her, that this was the last time she would be in bed with him ever again.

Ron eventually stirred, rousing from his sleep.

"Good Morning beautiful!" he said all smiles.

"Good Morning!" she mustered, not sure what else to say.

Ron took her hand, planting a single kiss in the middle of her hand, noticing the dark brown freckles dotted on her skin, he gently rubbed his stubbly chin over the freckles.

"Ron!" Jessica said shakily, her voice cracking. It pained her to utter her next words. "We can't do this again, I think its best that you leave now. You want to be her husband again right? So why are you in my bed?" she was upset. Upset with him for leaving her and upset with herself for letting him touch her again. "Don't call me, don't write me and don't text me, we can't chat, don't call to wish me happy birthday, don't call to see how I'm doing. Nothing," she said angrily. She looked away, she didn't want to cry in front of him.

Jessica noticed Ron was frowning, thick deep lines were embedded in his forehead. He said nothing, only squeezing her hand tightly in silent agreement.

"I'll have my things collected on Sunday," he said softly.

"Who's gonna pack your shit cause I'm not," she hissed at him.

"I'm not doing this to hurt you," his words were sincere. "I would have happily married you, but it just wasn't our time."

"Does she know about us?" she asked quizzically.

"She might. She's never asked me about you."

"I feel like I've wasted a year of my life playing house. If you wanted to screw me you could have told me that from day one." She wanted to hurt him just as much as he'd hurt her.

Ron scowled at her without any response.

He tossed the sheets aside, he picked his briefs from the floor and slid them on, he found his shirt and pants and dressed still glaring at her.

"I'm not that type of man, you should know that."

"What I do know is that you are a deceitful, lying ass son of a bitch and I'd like you to get the fuck out of my house."

"Don't you ever talk to me like that," he snarled.

"Or what Ron?" she said, challenging him. He once loved her feistiness but he did not need her shit right now.

"Bye Jessica," he abruptly turned on his heels and left the room. He had washed up in the guest bathroom and changed his clothing and stood in the hallway outside of her bedroom door. Jessica, still naked, grabbed her robe, flung it on and met his gaze from across the room.

A light sheen of sweat appeared on Jessica's arm. She rushed to her bathroom and closed the door. She sat on the floor and cried silently until she felt relief. The pain in her soul was unbearable. Why did she sleep with him? How dumb could she be?

Jessica stood and plucked her face rag from the towel rack, she soaked it with warm water from the tap and pressed it to her face, she wiped down her arms and neck. She cleaned the rag and returned it to the rod, she then brushed her teeth and returned to her bedroom. Ron was still standing by the door.

"What are you waiting for?" she said sullenly.

He nodded. He wanted to say more but he didn't. He walked back into the bedroom, embracing her gently for the last time. They stayed embracing each other for what seemed like eternity. In reality it was only a few seconds. He released her, stepped back to look at her, leaned in and kissed her on her lips. He then turned and walked out of the bedroom.

Jessica listened for the click of her front door and the roaring of Ron's car engine. Satisfied he was gone, she slowly sat down at the edge of her bed, emotionally drained. Tears which she tried to hold back threatened to escape her eyes regardless. Regaining some composure, she returned to bed, pulled her comforter tightly around her and rested her head onto her pillow.

A thousand thoughts rushed through her brain, bringing with it a tornado of a headache. She could hardly think straight. She allowed herself to cry her final cry as she fervently promised herself she'd never let another man break her heart again.

Jessica skipped work that Monday, feigning sickness, she really did feel sick but not how her boss would have thought. She simply just laid in bed all day until the hunger pangs became too unbearable. She popped into the kitchen, made a quick bowl of cereal, ate and dashed back to bed.

She thought of Ron, wondering whether he had already packed up and moved back to his marital home. Were his kids happy and excited to have him back? Was he still in love with his ex-wife? These thoughts were driving her crazy. She flipped on her bedroom tv searching for a movie to distract her thoughts.

She soon found something to watch on HGTV, she snuggled deeper into bed, surrounded by her many pillows, she was fascinated learning the ins and outs of home renovations.

The setting sun found Jessica snoring loudly, fast asleep. The television show had switched to flipping houses when she eventually stirred. Stretching, Jessica decided to call her sister Charmaine, she picked up the phone on her night stand and dialed. Better late than never she thought.

Charmaine arrived at 7:00 p.m. She pulled open the refridgerator door and grabbed a bottle of water. She was bedecked in her business attire, Jessica was instantly impressed.

"You look hot as hell ma'am, what's the occasion?" Jessica quipped coyly.

"I had an investment meeting today." Charmaine offered.

"So why did I need to come over tonight, what's so important?" she queried, sipping water from the bottle.

Jessica updated her sister, giving her all of the sordid details. Charmaine was stunned. When Jessica finished giving her the story, Charmaine was speechless. She gazed at her sister, again with her bug eyed expression.

Finally able to speak, Charmaine walked up to her Jessica and embraced her closely, while she, herself held back tears.

She slapped Jessica hard across her hand. "Ouch!" Jessica screamed.

"And why the hell did you sleep with him?"

"It just sorta happened," Jessica said guardedly.

Charmaine snorted totally disgusted with her sister.

"How are you coping, are you ok?"

"No. I'm not ok! I'm hurt and confused. I don't know what to do," she said as she played with the flowers on her kitchen Island, avoiding eye contact.

Sighing, "That's fucked up!" Charmaine continued. "What an A-hole."

Not to rile her sister up further, she informed Charmaine that with time, she'll be fine.

"It's a good thing you never got pregnant girl! That would be way worst and too complicated."

"So very true," Jessica agreed. "I'm still glad he told me before we got to the point where the consequences would have been detrimental for me," Jessica chimed in.

"What does his wife look like?" Charmaine asked full of attitude.

"How the hell would I know!" Jessica asked angrily. "I don't care what she looks like either."

"Uhmm hmm" Charmaine mused.

"Do you think he'll stay?"

"He's determined too I guess." Jessica was perturbed by her sister's comments.

"I think you dodged a bullet honestly. Yea he's hot and all but you never know with people."

Jessica made no acknowledgement of her sister's remark.

"Will you tell mom and dad?"

"Not yet. I need a few more days before I have **that** conversation," she sighed.

As they discussed Jessica's next steps, Charmaine's husband called her to find out why she was so late reaching home. She explained that she stopped by Jessica's and would be on her way shortly.

Ending their conversation, they promised to check in with each other as soon as possible and Jessica walked Charmaine to the door. They said their goodbyes and Jessica then laid on her couch replaying their conversation in her mind. She picked up her cell, put it back down, picked it up again and put it back down. She wanted to hear Ron's voice. However, she turned her cell off and decided to go to bed.

She switched her house lights off and went to bed early. She knew the next few days were going to be rough.

7

As promised, bright and early Sunday, Ron showed up with a truck and workers to haul his shit away. He barely gave her a low Good Morning as he invaded her space. She watched closely as the workmen ferried his belongings to the truck outside. She insisted that he got all of his shit in one swoop since he'd never be invited into her home again. He turned beet red but she didn't care, he obliged her and within an hour they were gone.

Jessica went insane, she lit some sage and sanitized and reorganized her home. When she was satisfied, she started breakfast and later cooked a light meal for her dinner. She then spent the rest of the day, relaxing and gossiping with Charmaine about Ron and his attitude when he collected his possessions.

The next few weeks were the toughest of Jessica's

life, between work and avoiding all thoughts of her failed relationship, she had her work cut out for her. She poured all her time and energy into her job, never taking a break. Her dedication did not go unnoticed; she was soon promoted to Senior Property Manager/Broker. Jessica thought things were finally looking up and she was totally elated.

As the weeks and months rolled on, she seldom thought of Ron, not that she didn't miss Ron, but, it made no sense dwelling on the past.

Charmaine being as nosy as she is, told Jessica one day during their usual lunch dates that Ron did move back in with his wife and they were seen around town.

"That's nice," she said coldly. Not caring to hear more details, she changed the conversation to something her stomach could handle.

Jessica started spending more time with her parents and siblings. She cooked for them and visited even more than she did before.

Telling her parents that she and Ron were no longer together was nerve wrecking, with Charmaine by her side for moral support, she once again relayed the details of her break up to her parents as fast as she could and fielded their questions with as much dignity as she could muster, her parents sensing her unease did not pressure her further, they hugged her and cried with her and then they prayed for her. Jessica hoped that that was the last time she was forced to relive her breakup story.

As the news spread within their inner couple, coupled with the fact that Ron was seen around town with his ex-wife and kids, tongues soon started wagging.

Jessica fielded many calls from her sisters and extended family once the news hit, it became so overbearing that she blocked certain numbers or simply ignored their calls. She even went as far as declining invitations to parties and dinners from her friends who thought the only way to get over a man was to get under another one. Jessica was in no way ready to date anyone.

Moving forward, Jessica felt a new zest for life. She was happy and content, her job was demanding but she loved every minute of it. She even started a new diet and was amazed at what healthy, clean eating was doing for her hair, skin and body.

She was at home, chilling on her patio. The sun was high and bright in the sky, it stung her face a little, intensifying the brownness of her gorgeous eyes. It was a lovely day, fanning herself, she took a sip of the cold lemonade she made earlier that morning. She decided to call her sister to see what she was doing on this particularly beautiful day.

"Hey sissy poo, what are you and the kids doing on this sunny day?" she asked cheerily.

"I am actually taking the kids to the beach, wanna join?" Charmaine asked.

"Don't mind if I do. Pick me up. What time are you leaving home?"

"I'll be there in 30 minutes. See you soon!"

Hanging up from her sister, Jessica skipped to her bedroom, flung open her swimsuit drawer searching for a hot bikini. Biting her lips, she mulled over her choices, she pulled the entire draw out, spilling the contents unto her bed. Sorting through her suits, she decided on a colourful 2 piece swimsuit, she paired it with white cut off shorts and tan flip flops. She showered quickly, styled her hair and added minimal makeup to her face. She was ready and excited.

She sat in her kitchen waiting for her sister to arrive idly flipping through an At Home magazine.

Bored, she walked to her huge mirror in the

hallway, checking herself out. Doing a 360 turn, she loved all her angles. Impressed with her super flat mid-section, toned thick thighs and big butt, she knew she was a sight to behold. Jessica began posing in the mirror, with one arm akimbo and one hand lightly planted on her forehead, she gave her best vogue magazine pose. She spinned and turned until she heard the horn of her Charmaine's car outside.

Giggling girlishly, she grabbed her purse, beach bag and bottled water and flew outside. She was elated to get out of the house. Jessica greeted her nephews and talked smack with Charmaine all the way to the beach. When they arrived they set up towels on the sand and paid for umbrellas and chairs from a local vendor.

On such a hot day, the beach was packed to capacity. Jessica took her sun screen from her bag and began to lather up her nephews, she then lathered up her legs, arms and stomach and asked Charmaine to lather her back. She returned the favour to her sister and then she laid back in her chair and smiled. The hot sun felt so good on her body.

"How do you like your new position at work?" Charmaine asked, sipping a bottle of cold water.

"It's awesome, I love what I do and it makes me content. I love helping people find their dream homes, watching the happy smiles on their faces. It's rewarding for me," she said thoughtfully

"How come huzzy didn't come?" she quizzed Charmaine.

"You know he hates the sun girl."

They both laughed.

Jessica and Charmaine watched the kids frolicking in the water.

"Have you heard from Ron?" she asked cautiously, observing her sister's reaction, she continued "I saw him four days ago, with his wife or ex-wife, whatever you wanna call it. He introduced me to her."

A gradual heat rose at the back of her neck. She turned her body slightly towards her sister just staring at her. After a few uncomfortable moments Charmaine continued, "Her name is Lydia," Charmaine continued describing Ron's wife to her. She really didn't want to hear it but she was enthralled, as Charmaine described in detail the circumstances of the introduction.

Jessica remained silent. Thankfully, the kids ran back to them for water and snacks, she laid flat again and gazed out at the sea. Charmaine took subtle glances at her sister as she fed the children.

After a few minutes of eating, the kids ventured a few feet away building sand castles in the sand.

In an attempt to not dampen the mood, Charmaine switched topics and focused the conversation on their parents, her newest celebrity client, grocery shopping and good movies they've both watched and money matters.

"Tai!" Don't throw sand in your brother's face. Charmaine bellowed at her older son.

"Okay mom!" he replied.

As the kids continued playing, Jessica scanned the beach noticing some serious eye candy, she wasn't ready to date but she wasn't blind. They were a few sexy men jogging or strolling on the beach; they were couples laid out together sunning, they were families drinking and chatting and they were singles. Everyone was out enjoying the hot sunny day.

Feeling to soak in the warm water, she stood, dropped her shorts and told her sister she was going for a dip and waded into the water.

Every available eye, both men and women, watched as Jessica entered the water. Jessica was always unaware of the way heads turned whenever she was present. She was drop dead gorgeous, a beautiful black goddess.

At 5:00 p.m. it was time to go. She slinked out of the water, back to beach chairs and her sister. Jessica and the boys toweled off, changed into dry clothes, cleaned up their empty snack bags and empty bottles, ensured they had everything and headed back to the car.

Charmaine dropped Jessica home. They said their goodbyes and she headed inside. Jessica's cell began ringing while she stripped and headed to take a shower.

It was Charmaine asking Jessica to tag along with her on a supermarket trip the next day. Jessica agreed then took a nice cool bath, when she emerged she grabbed the tv remote and sat on the couch, flipping through channels.

The conversation she had with her sister popped into her head. She couldn't help but wonder if Ron ever told his wife about her. Had she ever seen Jessica before? They probably passed each other on the street and didn't even know it. Did Ron miss her?

These thoughts roamed her mind for a few; she shook her head trying to force the torment from her mind. Picking something from the tv guide she settled in for the hour long movie.

Jessica dozed off five minutes after the movie started. Typical Jessica, the movie credits were rolling when she finally woke up.

Stretching, she felt starved. She filed into the kitchen and raided her cabinets, she set her ingredients on her kitchen island and started prepping for a simple meal. She found some large votive candles in the back of one of her kitchen cabinets and lit two; she centered them on her kitchen counter to create a relaxing ambiance while she cooked.

After her meal, she made her way to bed, she

switched off the tv, took her book with her and snuggled up with her pillows and continued reading well into the night.

Jessica slept straight through until morning only rising at 9:00 a.m., she ambled to the kitchen and started breakfast. She ate, showered, dressed and waited for Charmaine to pick her up once more.

While sipping on another cup of coffee, Charmaine arrived and they chatted about the great day they enjoyed at the beach the day before.

"I didn't mean to upset you yesterday by mentioning Ron," Charmaine said.

"It is what it is." Jessica shrugged.

"Is he still reaching out?" Charmaine asked.

"Nope," she offered.

"Ok. Let's go." Charmaine said.

They took off to the store. Charmaine was searching for a space as close as possible to the entrance; she bypassed three spots which were much further off.

"Girl! Just park," Jessica barked.

"Shut up and sit cho' ass down!" Charmaine shouted.

Charmaine circled the carpark twice more until she found a good spot.

Jessica was steaming.

"Every damn since, I hate driving with you," she said aggravated.

"Bitch, whatever, ughhh." Charmaine was irritated.

"Get us a cart." Charmaine said.

"Not for fuck, get it your damn self," Jessica hissed.

"What is wrong with you?" Charmaine asked exasperated.

Charmaine ignored her sister's funky attitude and grabbed a cart before heading inside.

They strolled through the aisles, selecting their purchases.

"Have you ever tried this cheese?" Jessica asked.

"No, you?" Charmaine replied.

"Nope, someone at work told me it's pretty good," she said.

Jessica chuckled to herself. She knew her sister was mad at her and ignoring her, she'd soon get over it, Charmaine knew that Jessica meant nothing by her antics.

"I need to get some vegetables," Charmaine added.

They made their way to the vegetable section. When they rounded the corner heading to the vegetable section, what they saw next, stopped them both in their tracks.

8

There was Ron. Ron, his ex-wife and their children. They were backing Jessica and Charmaine, at the refridgerator section viewing the wide selection of ice cream flavours.

Jessica stood there stunned, unable to move. She tapped Charmaine's shoulder and pointed in the direction of her former lover. Ron was such a handsome man, well groomed beard, broad chest, nice body; he was looking dapper in his sweat shirt and grey joggers. Seeing them together was surreal, as she turned to her ex-husband animatedly, Jessica caught a slight glimpse of her face; she was pretty, slender and curvy in a navy blue knee length dress and nude heels.

Before Jessica could look away from them, they abruptly turned, he was pushing their grocery cart slightly ahead. At that exact moment he glanced around and looked directly at Jessica. She jumped a little, startled that she was caught staring at him and his ex-wife.

Time seemed to stand still as their eyes connected. A strong ache enveloped Jessica. She wanted to break eye contact but she couldn't look away, Ron nodded his headed towards her and she nodded in return.

Charmaine linked her arm into her sister's arm and forced her to start walking. "Let's go," she said.

Shock and sadness were eating away at her core. She'd never seen them together before. Why did it surprise her so much? Why did she feel this way? What *was* she feeling? Feelings she thought were long gone.

She prayed she didn't see them again, they hurriedly finished their shopping and headed to the cashier booth, Jessica scanned the checkout line before proceeding forward, they cashed out and made their way to the car park.

Silence ensued. They loaded up the car, drove out of the car park and merged into the morning traffic.

"Are you ok?" Charmaine asked soothingly.

"I'm fine," she was not, neither did she feel like talking about it.

As Charmaine pulled up alongside Jessica's curb, Jessica detached her seatbelt, preparing to step out, she hesitated, looked towards her sister and began to cry. Charmaine unfastened her own seatbelt and leaned over to embrace her sister, she took her into her arms gently. Charmaine reaffirmed her love and devotion to her sister and gently stroked her shoulders repeatedly until her tears subsided.

"It's okay, sissy," she said, "I know, I know, I'm so sorry?" she said, trying to console her.

She kissed the top of Jessica's head, still holding her

tightly.

"I'm right here baby!" she listened as Jessica's sniffles abated.

"Why? Why did this have to happen to me?" Jessica asked dejectedly.

She felt so alone, even with her sister right there supporting and comforting her.

"Sadly, sometimes, that's just how life is. People come into our lives for a reason or a season, it was not God's will sissy, there is a man out there for you and only you," she offered. "You'll be fine."

"Thank you," she closed her eyes, regained her composure and then stepped out of the car. She removed her purchases from the car and said goodbye to Charmaine as she drove off.

Inside, Jessica dropped down unto her living room floor. She was disgusted with her reaction to seeing Ron and his family; it had now been almost one year since they broke up. She thought she was over him, seeing them together hit her like a ton of bricks. Closing her eyes again, she silently prayed to God for strength and endurance during this difficult moment. Jessica remained on the floor for hours, reeling in heartbreak.

Dragging herself off the floor, she retrieved her groceries from the hallway and packed them away; she placed her eggs and butter in the refrigerator and fish and meat in the freezer. With that chore completed, she ambled her way to her bedroom, threw her worn clothing in the hamper and showered longer than normal. Jessica allowed the very hot water to massage her neck and her back; she lathered, rinsed off her skin and stepped out. Snapping her robe from the hook, she pulled it on as she exited the bathroom.

Jessica sat on her bed and pulled her laptop closer, she needed to focus and not get flustered. She needed to prepare herself for a very important meeting she was to attend the next day. Feeling thirsty, she went into the kitchen for her favourite wine, she didn't even bother to grab a glass and instead, she took the whole bottle.

Two hours into work, she felt exhausted so she pushed the laptop aside and settled in for a little nap.

Jessica slept again until morning, her alarm sounded, waking her from her deep sleep. She stretched, tossed the covers off of her and started preparing for the day ahead.

As she walked to her car, she shook at her neighbours, said hello and slipped behind the wheel. Merging with traffic, she turned her radio volume up high, bopping her head to a sweet soca tune she'd never heard before from a new up and coming artiste.

After seven hours at work, the work day was finally over. Rush hour traffic was never fun, Jessica's commute was usually a thirty minute drive from her job to her home; she was stuck in traffic for two hours due to an accident on her route, finally, she was on her street; she parked, killed her engine and exited her car.

While checking her mailbox, she heard a familiar voice behind her.

"Jess, hey, how are you? I haven't seen you in a while?" It was her neighbour Trey; he was five foot nine, clean cut with a decent build, smooth dark chocolate skin and nice almond shaped eyes. Handsome. He reminded her of the actor Blair Underwood. Trey was one of the first neighbours she met when she moved into her home. Jessica had purchased her two storey, two bedroom, two bathroom bungalow one year after her first major job. She immediately fell in love with the décor; granite countertops, granite island, the beautiful fireplace and high ceilings and the sizable walk in closet in the master bedroom. It was Trey, who assisted her in transporting her personal property from her car to the house.

He came over that day, introduced himself and offered to help, and the rest as they say is history. He lived across the street from Jessica only a few houses down. They soon built a pleasant friendship and they often chatted online or had dinner at each other's homes.

"Heyyy Trey Ray!, Hello Maximus!" Max for short. Max was Trey's Golden Retriever, he was a big ass dog and Jessica always shunned him, he had an awful habit of jumping on her whenever he saw her.

"What are you doing out so late?" she asked. It was after 6:00 p.m.

"It's not that late ole' girl! he chided while laughing.

"True! So what brought you over?" she replied.

"I wanted to see if you wanted to have dinner Friday night, if you aren't too busy?"

"I don't have any immediate plans. I'll confirm, maybe Wednesday?" she asked eyebrows raised.

"Cool! If you don't let me know, I'm gonna come over anyway," he laughed as Max sped off dragging him behind.

Trey was a very cool dude and they usually shared good times together.

The week flew by and after several meetings with clients, viewings and reports compiled. Jessica was beat.

At home that Friday, Jessica completely forgot about her 'potential' dinner with Trey. While she was chilling out on her couch, there was a knock at her door. Jessica was in no mood for visitors plus she wasn't expecting anyone so she ignored the knocking.

Hoping the person caught the drift and left, she settled back down. There were three more knocks. Annoyed, she angrily rushed to the door, she was ready to cuss the person out. Spying through the peephole she recognized who it was. She spotted Trey's brown Mohawk styled hair, shit she thought, she forgot about him.

Jessica opened the door. Smiling, she said, "I'm so sorry. I forgot!"

Trey stood there, a cooling bag in hand and a big smile on his face. He smelled so good. Uhmmm.

"I did say I was gonna show up if you didn't confirm."

"Come on in," she extended her arm ushering him in.

Trey set up dinner in the dining room while she took the plates and wine glasses from the cabinet and began laying out the cutlery.

Over dinner, Trey told Jessica that he heard about the breakup between her and Ron.

"How are you coping with everything?" he asked apprehensive at first.

Shrugging, she said "I'm ok yuh know...it's been a process. When we first broke up, it was rough. I'm...I'm cool now. It's been awhile though." Jessica took a sip of wine and set her glass down.

"What about you? Are you seeing anyone?" she countered.

"Nah. Not right now."

"Are you interested in dating?" he asked.

Jessica chewed her food slowly, mulling over his question.

"I'm not ready, I don't know when I'll be ready. Honestly, I never want to experience that pain again."

"Hmmm" Trey uttered.

"You hmm a lot, what's that about?" Jessica said jokingly.

"Nothing," he said. "How about going out with me?" Trey was serious. He really liked Jessica.

"On a date?" Jessica queried.

"Not on a date date," he was smiling from ear to ear, "Would you be interested in dating me?"

"As sweet as you are Trey, I'm not ready to start dating right now. I don't mind us hanging out," Jessica was flattered but she was scared to date.

Trey picked up his wine and took a big gulp. Dinner went smoothly and Jessica was quite surprised that she was enjoying his company so much. Trey and Jessica cleaned up after dinner and Jessica invited him to sit on the patio where a cool night breeze was cascading down from the hills. She took her throw from her couch in the event it got extremely cold.

Two bottles of wine later, they were still on the patio. Jessica learned that Trey served in the military eight years ago straight out of high school, he relocated to the suburbs after his contract had expired, jobs were few and far between but he was determined to succeed; he went back to school, obtained his construction and engineering degree, applied for a loan and started his own successful construction company.

Jessica was very captivated with his story.

They ended the evening on a fantastic note, they promised to get together again soon.

Jessica thanked him for dinner and walked him to the door. She watched him stroll back over to his home, where he turned and waved. Jessica waved back and returned to her couch.

Jessica was quite happy that Trey came over, a pleasant interruption. Trey was an attractive man, she mused. She peered between her legs, "down girl," she said out loud. She looked forward to their next dinner.

9

For the next few months Jessica threw herself into work.

She also stopped refusing invitations to events and started socializing, she didn't realize how much she missed the nightlife. She often saw Ron at certain events, they simply nodded towards each other, that was it, words were never spoken between them. Jessica was no longer upset with him, in a way; she understood why he ended his relationship with her.

Trey would often come over for dinner or just to watch television and catch up, there was always an undeniable chemistry between them. They both felt it.

Jessica invited her parents over one weekend, she was so busy that her parents were complaining about not seeing her. She felt guilty so she'd invited them over for lunch. Jessica made a healthy lunch of grilled fish and salad and set the table. She invited her sisters but they were all busy, or so they said. Jessica knew her sisters wanted to avoid the wrath they were going to lay down on her. Anyway, she wasn't upset, she had it all under control.

"I saw Ron and his ex-wife together at the grocery store," she informed them. Jessica's parents were still salty about the breakup when she first told them; they too were distraught over the news.

"What happened?" they asked, eager to hear more.

"Nothing really, we just looked at each other and that was it."

"I hope you didn't let it bother you," her mother said sternly.

"It did at first, but then I prayed and pushed through it and eventually I got over it."

"Who is she?" her dad asked.

"Her name is Lydia, that's all I know."

"God has a better man for you baby, take your time to heal, don't rush into anything with anyone," her father said.

"Yes daddy." Jessica loved her parents immensely.

The conversation changed direction to Jessica's upcoming 29th birthday. She intended on hosting an intimate dinner with friends and family. She would extend an invitation to a few close colleagues and Trey. They chatted idly about venues, the décor and the food, she promised to let them know if she needed any assistance with the bill. She was doing pretty well financially but she accepted their offer, she didn't want to hurt their feelings. As her parents were preparing to leave, Jessica packed them two containers of food to cover them for at least the next day.

They kissed and hugged each other goodbye and

she watched them bundling into their car from her doorway. Jessica hugged herself closely against the chilly night wind, while standing on the edge of the doorway. Closing the door behind her, she entered her kitchen, removed the used wine glasses, tossing them and the dirty dishes into the dishwasher and then wiped the dinner table down.

Settling in for the night, Jessica decided to get in a little exercise. Even though she was in very good shape, she wanted to look her very best for her birthday. Thirty minutes later, Jessica was still panting as she went through a grueling High-Intensity Interval Training workout she found on YouTube. With her workout complete, she was proud of her endurance. She didn't quit as the workout intensified, she kept pushing, focusing on her end game. Drenched in sweat from head to toe, she lugged her sore body to her shower and filled the tub and soaked the soreness away.

Drying off after her soak, she pulled a sexy nightie from her drawer, dressed and headed to the kitchen. There she made a snack of peanut butter celery sticks and took a bottle of water back to her bedroom. Hauling her sore body onto the bed, she switched the tv on in her room and started nibbling on her healthy snack. A flashing blue light beneath the covers of the bed alerted Jessica that her cell was ringing. "Trey!" she was beaming.

"Buenos Noches!" Jessica said sweetly, smiling from ear to ear.

Laughing he said "I have no idea what that means," they both cracked up laughing.

"It means good evening in Spanish," she offered.

"I noticed that you were at home and I wondered if you wanted to chill for a while," he asked.

Jessica considered his offer.

"Sure. I'll leave the door unlocked."

Jessica dashed to her front door and unlocked it, she dashed back up the stairs and slipped off her sexy nightie and opted for pajama sweats, she checked her reflection in her vanity mirror and rushed to her living room.

Trey entered two minutes later.

"Wow," he breathed. He was taken aback by Jessica's natural beauty.

"Wow what?" she asked, knowing exactly what he meant.

"You look awesome!" he said, flashing perfect teeth.

"Thank you," she said, not breaking eye contact with Trey. Jessica was school girl giddy.

"How come you're up this late?" he continued.

"Burning the midnight oil just like you," she said.

Leading him to the couch, they sat directly next to each other.

Trey found the tv remote and flipped to a sports channel.

Trey was a persistent man and he was not going to give up so easy in pursuing Jessica.

Jessica took a beer from the refridgerator and gave it to Trey, since she was on a diet, she sipped on a bottle of water.

Jessica and Trey settled in to watch a football game on tv. Trey explained certain plays to Jessica that she didn't understand and pointed out his favourite player. She was not an avid sports fan but she was content to let him display his knowledge of the sport.

Jessica soon got bored watching the game. She asked him to play a game of scrabble and he obliged, peeping occasionally at the tv screen as they played.

They were both having fun. Jessica beat him unmercifully, a fact which he graciously accepted.

He soon had to go. Jessica wasn't ready for the night to end but she had work to get too also.

"Before you go, I'm having my birthday party on the August 21st, would you like to be my plus one?" she asked cautiously.

"Damn sure, I'll gladly be your plus one," he answered excitedly.

"Cool. It's at 6:00 p.m. So you can pick me up at 5:00 p.m. It's down in the city at the Angels Birch Banquet Hall. Do you know where that is?"

"Yes, I've passed there a few times...fancyyy" he said eyebrows raised.

Jessica playfully swatted him on his shoulder.

"You play too much," she retorted.

She walked him to the door and watched him walk over to his home.

The next day, Jessica began finalizing the details of her birthday dinner. Her party planner submitted a wide range of décor ideas from which she was to select her preferred colour schemes and table settings ideas and email those back to her. Jessica also hired a renowned caterer and had an appointment early the next day to sample the menu that would be served. She also secured an elaborate banquet hall with magnificent gardens, which she intended to use to take photos with her family and friends.

Those tasks done, she gathered her purse and laptop and headed to a showing she scheduled in the country side. It was a three bedroom luxury apartment which she really wanted to sell. It was on the market for ten months and her boss really wanted it gone. The week flew by and Jessica could not wait for her birthday dinner/party, it was scheduled to start at 6:00 p.m., she was super excited. She received updates throughout the week from her party planner and everything was confirmed.

That Friday evening, she visited the salon, got her hair pressed straight, her nails and toes polished and her lashes refreshed. Perfect. She returned home, undressed and gave her body a nice soak in the tub, careful not to get her hair wet. When she felt the water getting cold, she stepped out and pulled the stop plug to release her bath water.

Hanging from her closet door was the sexy number which she intended to wear. It was a red, sparkly, off-the-shoulder, high split dress that fit her body like a glove. It accentuated every curve that she owned. She trailed her finger over the fabric, rubbing her fingers over the sparkly gems. Satisfied, she began beating her face to perfection. Angling her face in the mirror, she checked that her hair, eye liner, mascara, lipstick and foundation were all applied seamlessly.

When she was finished she turned to her dress. She glided the dress up her thighs and over up breasts. The dress was long, right down to her ankles and she loved it. She spun around in the mirror admiring her physique.

Trey would soon be there, happy that he was her date for the evening.

Ensuring she had everything in her purse: mints, gum, lipstick, cell and keys. She was all set.

Instantly, there was a knock on the door. That must be Trey.

Stepping in to her red heels, she sashayed to the door.

She opened the door and Trey could not keep his composure.

"Dammnnnnn, Ms. Clarke you look gorgeous," he said lustfully. She was a vision.

"Thank you. Much appreciated," she said coyly.

Stepping through the door, Trey took Jessica by the

hand and slowly spinned her around, admiring all that was before him. Wow, he thought.

Releasing her, he happily followed behind her. They stepped out to the car and made it to the hall within twenty minutes.

"You look absolutely amazing!" he said, sneaking her glances as he drove.

"Thank you. You look very dapper also." Jessica had blown Trey's mind and she was freaking out inside. They chatted all the way to the venue, he was nervous and was praying he didn't do anything to offset her on her special night. As they entered the parking area, she greeted some of her invited guests, who were all dressed up to the nines.

Trey parked and came around to the passenger side of the car to open the door for Jessica. After all it was her night. They walked hand in hand and Jessica greeted other guests as they approached the entrance to the venue. Inside she greeted her mum and dad, her sisters, Charmaine, Olivia, Alexus, Rebecca and Ashley. Everyone was stunned by the visual Jessica presented.

All of her sisters were fussing over her and she was every bit of the attention. Jessica took the opportunity to introduce Trey to her family and friends. Trey was told how lucky he was by practically all of the dinner party, they all knew of the heartbreak she suffered during her break up with Ron so they wished her the best but advised her to proceed with caution.

At 6:45 p.m., everyone was asked to be seated as dinner commenced.

The hall where the birthday dinner was being held was filled with animated chatter as the courses were shared.

Laughter and conversation were the order of the

night and Jessica was busy eating and chatting with Trey and those around her. The food so far was delicious, she thought.

The final course was being served when her dad stood to give a special tribute to his daughter. Mr. Clarke recalled how, when Jessica was five years old, he caught her in his closet eating a big tub of icecream she somehow got from the kitchen counter. Laughing, he further recalled a 15 year old Jessica's first fight at school. His proudest moment was her graduating university with her business degree. In conclusion he expressed his love and affection for her. Jessica blew a kiss to her dad when he was finished.

The dessert was an immaculate red velvet cake. Supple and moist, Jessica ate two slices. She would have to burn the calories off with intense cardio. Mingling among her guests, she shared memories from high school, to part time jobs to university. With the evening winding down, the photographer was ready to do his job. The entire dinner party followed them to the garden to watch as the photos were taken.

Between him running back and forth showing her the images as they were taken and Jessica changing poses, they stood in the garden for at least an hour and thirty minutes. By 11:00 p.m. some guests were leaving and a few remained in the garden, Jessica grabbed more wine and she and Trey separated from the other guests to chat alone. After another forty-five minutes, it was time to say goodnight.

Jessica had a quick word with her party planner, she thanked the caterer and Dj for their professionalism and for making her dinner a success. She handed each individual their final cheques and returned to her date. She said goodnight to her remaining guests and wished them all a safe trip home.

Trey helped her pack her birthday gifts into the car

and then headed home.

She placed the gifts on her kitchen counter and she and Trey both plopped down on her couch, she was tired but too excited to sleep so she switched on the tv. He took Jessica's hand in his as he simultaneously grabbed the remote with his other hand and muted the tv, turning slightly to face Jessica, he cleared his throat as if he wanted to speak.

"I really like you Jessica!" he stated.

"Trey...," she began.

Trey stopped her mid-sentence. "Let me finish," he said softly.

"I know you said that you weren't ready for a relationship. I respect that. I'm not trying to force you into anything. I simply want to know where your head is at?"

Jessica paused before responding.

"I really like you too. I'm just afraid. You know?" Jessica tried to remain as emotionless as possible, "I never thought I'd find myself here again," she said.

As they held hands on the couch Trey leaned in closer.

Jessica felt as though her chest would explode, she didn't know what to do.

Their lips touched, their lips parted and they kissed. Jessica felt stirrings deep within her that she hadn't felt in almost eighteen months, fireworks were exploding between her legs. Her hands lightly rested on his arms as she titled her head slightly, enjoying each moment as his tongue did its own dance expertly inside of her mouth. She was in heaven.

Breaking apart, they both smiled sheepishly.

"I'm sorry," he was embarrassed. He didn't want to push her away because of his actions.

"It's ok," she said, resting her forehead against his,

she closed her moist eyes, fear and uncertainty gripping her.

"I enjoyed kissing you," she looked up into his eyes. She wasn't afraid of him at all. The uncertainty of it all was crushing her heart like a pressurized cooker. Jessica snuggled up to Trey, enjoying the way he caressed her. Trey unmuted the tv and they sat there intertwined enjoying the moment, each silently wondering what next.

10

Jessica could not sleep. Once again her mind was running rampant thinking of Trey. After Trey left, she switched off her lights and retreated to her bedroom. Would he treat her right? Would he love her unconditionally? Would she make him happy? Jessica pulled her pillow on top of her face and screamed into it.

Finally, it was morning. Still team 'no sleep', she headed to the kitchen and flicked the switch for the coffee machine. She loved the gurgling sound the machine made while sputtering out her coffee, popping the refrigerator door open; she opted for eggs and toast. The aroma of her breakfast cooking penetrated her nostrils. She was hungry.

Jessica decided to tidy up a little before heading out for the day. As she fluffed the pillows of her couch, she recalled the kiss she and Trey shared. She made a mental note to call him later that day.

Jessica sat in her office chair unpacking her ordered lunch. Still on her health kick, she ordered a Greek salad and an iced tea from a restaurant two blocks down from her office. Diving in, she stretched across her desk attempting to pull her desk phone closer, she punched in Trey's cell number while she munched on her delicious salad.

"Good Evening, this is Trey Sommers."

Trey's voice was super sexy, she was instantly turned on.

"Good Evening handsome, are you busy?" she asked.

"Good Evening beautiful," he replied, "I'm happy you called, you've been on my mind all week."

"It's my pleasure," she said seductively.

Jessica removed the phone from her mouth and bent over snickering, careful not to let him hear her.

"When am I going to see you next?" she asked as she pushed her food around.

"Tonight?" Trey held his breath eagerly awaiting her response.

"It's a date. Dinner is on me. See you at 7:00 p.m.?" she asked.

"7 stat!" he said.

"See you then, handsome," she responded.

"I can't wait to see you baby," he said suggestively.

Jessica ended the call and called her sister next.

Charmaine was backed up at work with clients. She promised to get back to her after work.

Jessica finished her lunch and was soon called into her boss' office to discuss a complaint he received from a client. Jessica explained in detail the circumstances surrounding the complaint and provided a palpable solution to the satisfaction of her boss and the client. Two hours later she was on her way out the door to the grocery store to purchase the supplies for dinner.

Attempting to make one trip, she hauled and heaved all the groceries from her car trunk to her front door, barely making it inside, she dashed to the kitchen before the weak plastic bags exploded spilling the contents everywhere.

Wiping the sweat from her brow with the back of her hand, she began shelving her purchases, including two new bottles of wine which she placed on the kitchen counter.

The next day started as usual; shower, breakfast, work. This time, she had something to look forward too. Jessica could not wait until she finished with work to get home to prepare dinner for her and Trey.

She spent the majority of her day eye balling the clock. She had already alerted her boss that she was leaving at 3:00 p.m. Not wanting to bring attention to the fact that she was leaving work early, she gathered her purse and slipped her boss a reminder note.

Parking on the curb outside of her home, she took her mail from the mailbox, briefly scanning the contents: bills, banking brochures and snail mail, she dropped them on the side table at the entrance of the hallway until she had time to review them later.

Changing out of her work wear, she slipped on a pair of blue shorts and khaki top and strolled to the kitchen. Pulling out pots and pans, Jessica started to prepare her famous grilled chicken, rice, steamed veg and apple pie for dessert.

By 6 p.m., dinner was complete.

Taking a 15 minute nap, she rose, showered and sat in front of her vanity.

Jessica studied her reflection once again, she smoothed her hands over her face searching for any imperfection. Pretty satisfied, she began styling her hair, deciding to leave it curly and loose. Hair approved, she applied her makeup and added sparkly silver earrings and her silver necklace and ring set, a gift from her mother, she then added a few splashes of perfume and retreated to the kitchen. She chose a red cold shoulder ankle length dress, which displayed her curves magnificently.

Jessica was truly a stunner.

At 6:45 p.m. she set the table and placed one bottle of wine into the wine cooler and set it on the table. She took the grilled chicken from the grill and placed each dish on the table.

At 7:00 p.m., she heard the knock on the door, she breathed deeply, her hand pressed firmly to her stomach, she exhaled, stood upright and sashayed to the door.

Smiling, she slowly opened the door.

"Oh my gosh. Wow! You look so good" he said in awe.

"You don't look too bad yourself!" she said playfully.

Trey was amazed at how gorgeous Jessica looked.

"Come on in," she said.

"Uhmm in here smells enticing," he said sniffing the air.

"Thank you."

Trey was looking dapper as hell tonight. Jessica was ecstatic.

Seating him next to her at the table, she indicated that he could pop the wine. He poured both of their glasses as Jessica plated the food.

The conversation was intellectual and entertaining. He wanted to know more about her; she offered more insight into her job, her likes and dislikes, her favourite books, wine and movies.

"What about kids?" he probed.

"Of course I want kids," she said giggling.

"Do you?" she queried.

"All boys for me. Two the max!" he said slyly.

"I'm fine with that," she said looking at him directly.
The atmosphere was thick with sexual tension.

Jessica took a big gulp of her wine to quell the
savage beast roaming her body.

"Hmmmm," she hung her head back and rolled her
neck from side to side, trying to control her
uncomfortable excitement.

"On a serious note," he started, recapturing her
attention.

"I have a business trip coming up soon, would you
care to join me? His eyes darkened irresistibly.

"I'm not sure, what type of trip?" Jessica crossed her
legs, squeezing them tight beneath her dress.

"A colleague of mine has a housing project he's
asking me to invest in. He invited me to come up and
view the land, go over some specs and meet with a few
other contractors," he said taking swig of wine.

"It's only for the weekend so you wouldn't be away
too long. Think about it and let me know."

Jessica agreed to think about taking the trip. She
could use a small vacation.

As they ate and chatted, she realized that she greatly
enjoyed his company, their conversations always flowed
naturally and he was always respectful and courteous.

"That was a great meal, thank you for the invite."

"You're welcome," she said.

"How about some dessert?"

"I'll have some of you any time of the day," he said
winking at her.

"Boyyy if you don't stop. You can't handle all this
sugar anyway," she winked back. Her panties were
soaked.

They piled the dishes into the sink and retreated to the couch, dessert in hand.

Snuggling close together, she rested her head on his arm. They couldn't resist. Propping her chin up to him, he kissed her urgently, pressing his lips to hers. Inhaling his essence was enough to drive Jessica crazy, she wanted more and so did he. He felt so strong, so masculine, she moaned into his mouth and she whispered "Take me upstairs."

Lifting her up gently from the couch, taking her up the stairs, he breathed in between kisses "Where?" she pointed and he followed her direction.

Oh my Gosh, was she ready for this? Yes. She was.

Stopping only to remove all their clothes, Jessica laid seductively on the bed. She was a beautiful woman.

Trey stripped naked and kneeled on the bed, he hovered over her for a moment, his eyes exploring and burning images of her naked body into his brain, Jessica spread her legs apart and stroked her moist slit in anticipation of what was to come, she could feel the slippery slickness of her juices on her fingertips. Trey leaned over her and kissed her passionately while she slowly fingered her clit, she eagerly stretched her hand between her legs and stroked his shaft rhythmically, his low moans echoing inside her of her mouth as his lips smashed against hers.

A pulsating need burned through his swollen shaft as he entered her. "Shit," she said as the gradual pressure of his thickness slid deep into her slit. Jessica felt her walls shiver as he increased his speed and rammed into her wetness ferociously, he was fucking her so good it took everything in her not to scream out loud, "Ohhh shit," was all she managed to say, she squirmed and quivered as his deep strokes ravaged her centre, he then started licking and sucking her swollen nipples, driving her crazy. Just as she was about to climax, he sat upright and pushed her legs to her chest and hungrily lapped at juices her with his tongue, savoring every last drop,

"Fuck," she hissed, with her legs pressed against her chest, she was powerless, he had all control over her and attacked her slippery slit hungrily, her cries were now uncontrollable as her walls contracted intensely and her hips bucked wildly against him. "Fuck Jessica, I'm gonna come," barely escaped his lips before a rush of hot cum squirted deep inside of her, his hips swirled and danced vigorously as he rammed his full length deep into her delicate slit repeatedly, a squealing groan rumbled from Trey as he shuddered and squirted everything in him inside of her, Jessica slammed her head back into the bed as her body jerked against the shock waves of intense pleasure sailing through her slit to her legs, The last thing she remembered before zoning out was the soft pitter patter of rain tapping on her window.

Propping up on her elbows, Jessica realized the sun was high. She was late for work.

The rustling next to her almost made her bolt from the bed. Looking over she smiled as she remembered the mind blowing events of last night.

Trey was still knocked out.

Mindful of the dreaded 'morning breath' she rushed to the bathroom to brush her teeth and slid back under the covers and gave him a quick peck on the lips.

Trey stirred.

"Good Morning beautiful," he said as he stretched.

"Good Morning," she replied, all smiles.

"Last night...I"

"Interrupting him, she blurted "Last night was perfect."

They shared one more passionate kiss. Jessica

pulled away, reminding him she was already late for work.

She removed the covers and headed to the bathroom.

Hopping from the bed, Trey grabbed her and pulled her back to bed. He straddled her, kissing her neck, trailing kisses between her breasts. Familiar stirrings swathed her and a robust heat spread across her entire womanhood. She moaned "Trey, wait!" He didn't. Trailing kisses between her thighs. Jessica closed her eyes. He stopped. "Let's continue in the shower."

Finishing what he started, he devoured her under the warm water. Jessica could hardly stand. Trey delighted in making her squirm, scream and cry. He held her firmly as she experienced climax after climax. When they were both sated, they toweled off and laid in bed exhausted.

After a few slow playful kisses they realized they were both starving, so they ordered in and stayed in bed.

While waiting for their delivery, Jessica called into work and made excuses for being late, she asked the receptionist to reschedule her appointments for later in the evening.

By the time she hung up the phone, breakfast had arrived.

They ate and caressed each other like horny teenagers.

Bellies full, they planned a date night soon. Trey playfully tapped Jessica on her butt, kissed her goodbye and made his way home. He was also late for work.

Jessica couldn't wait to update Charmaine on her date with Trey.

11

That afternoon during lunch, she called her sister and gave her the full rundown. Jessica did not spare any details. As she concluded the story, she mentioned Trey's invite and asked whether she should go.

"What do you have to lose?" she asked.

"Nothing!" Jessica added thoughtfully.

"Then go for it."

"Can you see a future with Trey?" Charmaine asked.

If Jessica was honest with herself, she'd also thought long and hard of a future with Trey.

"Yes I do. Honestly. He's everything I've desired."

"I'm so happy for you sissy. I pray it works out. But, take your time and enjoy the ride. Yuh know, like you did the other night."

"I sure will." Jessica busted out laughing.

Jessica made one more call.

"Good Afternoon...." Jessica cut him off.

"I'll go with you to New York!" Jessica waited nervously.

"I can't wait baby. We are gonna have a wonderful time."

For the next two months, following their trip to New York, Jessica and Trey planned weekly date nights, spending most of those nights together. They had gotten much closer. They even discussed casually getting married and having kids. Where would they live? Where would their kids go to school?

Their relationship was on the right track. He also took her to Barbados to meet his parents, it was an amazing trip. Jessica enjoyed meeting his family and his only brother, Samuel. His mother cooked a number of Barbadian delicacies that were absolutely delicious. Both she and Trey promised to return as soon as possible.

Trey was a little emotional saying goodbye to his parents. Jessica was happy to be there to offer support to Trey. Packed and ready to go, they awaited their taxi. When it arrived, there was barely enough room to hold them and their luggage.

While at the airport, they checked in and sat hand in hand waiting for their flight to be called. By the time the plane landed, they were tired and hungry again. Trey paid to retrieve his car from airport parking and headed to a small café on the outskirts of the airport. After lunch, they drove directly home, he dropped Jessica off and helped her unload her luggage before driving into his parking garage.

Closing and locking her door, she slumped to the floor. She rested there until she felt the need to relieve herself. Struggling from the floor, she got up and used her guest bathroom. She took her laptop from her luggage and she signed into her Gmail account, browsing her emails; the photographer she hired was supposed to send her the photos from her birthday dinner.

Scanning the names in her inbox, she found it. She opened the email and the photos began downloading by the click of a link. Jessica inspected every photo with a fine tooth comb. They were a few she hated but the majority were fantastic. She smiled looking at photos of her and her mom and dad and close friends. She stopped scrolling when she landed on one of her and Trey, she could definitely spend the rest of her life with him; she decided to use their photo as her profile pic via the social media App WhatsApp.

As the App updated her profile pic, she placed her phone on the hallway desk while dragging her luggage to the bedroom. She began sorting clothing for laundry and returning her jewelry and shoes from the trip to their boxes. She then stripped and showered, she also texted Trey and retired to bed. While scrolling through her messages on the same App, her phone vibrated indicating an incoming call. She answered without looking at the display.

"Hello. That's a very cute pic," Ron commented.

Jessica was almost certain she had blocked and deleted him.

"Isn't he your neighbor?"

"Didn't I tell you to drop dead?" Jessica was becoming increasingly irritated.

"Are you sleeping with him?" he persisted.

"Be worried about your wife and kids, not me." Jessica was pissed.

"I'm just asking?"

"No!" she practically screamed in his ear. "You don't have the right to ask me who I'm sleeping with," she replied back.

"You look happy," he continued.

"Fuck you," she said disgusted. Jessica ended the call and threw the phone on the floor. She flew off the bed, picked up the phone again and immediately blocked and deleted that number. She went to the kitchen, poured a shot of Hennessey and downed it one gulp. She was enraged, the gall of this negro, how dare he grill her after dropping her like a bad habit. Too upset to do anything else. She went outside for a walk around the neighbourhood.

Two hours later, she was still in a foul mood.

Trey appeared just as she was unlocking her door. He invited her over to his home. Jessica had spent many nights with Trey. It was the typical bachelor pad, black stark furniture, nothing pretty or interesting. No flowers. No Plants and not many photos. She was not there to critique his home, she needed to be comforted.

"What's wrong baby?" he asked genuinely concerned.

She shrugged.

She walked up to him, opened his arms and stepped into them. Sensing she was emotional about something, he squeezed her tightly in his arms and rocked her gently until he felt her body relax. Leading her to his living room they sat side by side still holding each other.

"Do you want to talk about it?" he asked.

She shook her head 'No'.

Jessica looked into his eyes, she began kissing him passionately, she had an itch that needed to be scratched, they moved the show to his bedroom and ended the night with a bang, they made love twice that night to the contentment of Jessica. She awoke startled by an unfamiliar wet sensation on her fingers. Her eyes flew open. Max was licking her fingers.

"Ewww Max. No," she shooed him away.

Jessica got up and went to the bathroom, she washed her hands and opened a new toothbrush she took from his cabinet. She brushed her teeth and washed her face and then went to the kitchen to see what Trey was doing since he was not in bed.

"Good Morning!" she said sweetly, she gave him a light peck on the cheek.

"Good Morning sleepy head," Trey was making a breakfast of bacon and eggs.

"In here smells delicious," her stomach was growling.

She took a mug from the counter, rinsed it with plain water and filled it with fresh coffee. The warm liquid was soothing to her stomach. While they ate breakfast, they discussed their schedule for the day and made plans to meet during the next few days.

Jessica walked to her home and quickly prepped for work. She was ready in 15 minutes.

Pulling into her designated parking spot, she saw one of her colleagues, getting out of his car.

"Good Morning Jessica," he enjoyed flirting with Jessica.

"Good Morning Bryan," she said dryly.

Bryan had always been attracted to Jessica. She never gave him the time of day. She, however, always remained cordial to him. She tossed her purse over her shoulder, tucked her folder beneath her arm, locked her car and wished him a great day and made her way inside.

"I'm stuck on a few accounts, can we discuss those later today? The boss said I should get your insight," he asked while trailing behind her, enjoying the view.

"Sure," she smiled, hiding her annoyance. "I'm free around 11:00 a.m."

"Cool. See you later then."

They separated to their individual offices. She checked with reception for any new messages or calls. Making herself comfortable in her office chair, she took her laptop, made a few clicks and opened up her Microsoft Excel spreadsheet and began updating her database. It was mandatory that all of her accounts be updated to show the current and correct status of all accounts assigned to her. Jessica's week was hard, between showing three condos and completing several property valuations, she was exhausted by weekend.

Jessica slept in Saturday morning. Around noon, she stretched, dragged herself to the kitchen, poured a cup of juice from the refridgerator and took it back to bed. She turned the tv on, Family Feud was showing, she laughed at the contestants while she drank her juice. She placed the empty glass on her nightstand and snuggled under the covers.

12

A sudden downpour of rain awakened Jessica from her light snooze. She rolled over on her stomach, positioning herself in line with the perfect views outside of her window. She loved the sound of the rain as it splattered on the roof, the sky was dark gray. It was going to be a rainy day.

Straining her neck to see the clock on the wall, she saw it was 1:00 p.m. in the afternoon. It was definitely time for lunch. She searched her drawer, found the flyer from the Seafood Hut and dialed the number. After placing her order, she resumed watching the tv, changing the channel to Lifetime's tv show Hoarders.

Within forty minutes, her doorbell chimed, she ran downstairs and peered through the peephole. She snatched the money from her purse and opened the door. It was Julie.

"Hey Ju Ju Bean girl," she said openly giggling.

"Hmmm. Sexy." Julie said flirting heavy. Jessica was standing there in a simple shorts and top and Julie was very attracted to her and always flirted with her. She kept it casual never fully over the top.

Jessica was not into women, but she did enjoy their flirty exchanges.

"I haven't seen you around!" Julie said.

"You wanted to see me?" Jessica said flirting back.

"Everyday of my life."

"Girl I can't with you. Hand me my lunch please." Jessica was rolling. Julie was a trip.

Jessica took her lunch and handed Julie her payment along with a generous tip.

Julie counted out the money, "Thank you sweetness. If you ever change your mind, you know where to find me." She blew Jessica a kiss and walked backwards towards her car, keeping her eyes on Jessica.

"You wouldn't know what to do with it if I gave it to you," she shouted to Julie.

"Try me." She walked away snickering.

Jessica waved bye and went back to her bedroom and dug right in.

She ate until she was full and uncomfortable. The lobster and corn were delicious, she didn't fancy the potatoes but downed everything else. She threw the container in the trash can in her bedroom until later when she would dump it in the garbage can in the kitchen. Since she was up, she took a shower, brushed her teeth and slipped back into the bed; she called her parents and caught up with them and then Charmaine. She made a call to Trey and he was coming over after he took care of his obligations at home.

Trey came over finally and snuggled up with Jessica in bed.

"Hello baby," he landed a wet kiss on her forehead.

"What took you so long?"

"I took Max for a quick walk and then I did some work and now I'm here."

"I hardly see you anymore," Jessica said glumly.

"I know, how about we take a 'baecation'. Take a couple days off," he said stroking her hand. "Since we've working so hard, we deserve it."

"I'd really like that," she said playing with the hair on his arm.

They discussed the best available dates and where they wanted to go.

"How about Cabo San Lucas? I've always wanted to go there. I heard it's gorgeous."

"Cabo it is," he ran his hand over her smooth thighs.

"Hand me my laptop please." She began browsing the internet for flights and hotels in Mexico. She wanted one close to the beach and maybe a Jacuzzi on their balcony.

"This looks cute," she angled the laptop so that Trey could see, he shaked his head in agreement. Jessica would make the final arrangements tomorrow. She rested the laptop on the floor and laid down across his chest.

"I love you."

They'd never said these three little words to each other before. They've implied it but never fully said it.

"I love you too." She never thought she'd ever utter those words again.

They kissed feverishly, hands roaming freely, touching, feeling and caressing. Clothing was tossed to the floor and an intense lovemaking session began. Jessica loved to feel his muscular, strong body on top of her. She arched her back as he rammed his engorged erection inside of her filling her to capacity. She clasped her hands around his neck as he nibbled and kissed her lips, pleasure radiated throughout her body. Trey flipped her over and she braced herself on her hands and knees as he slammed into her from behind, within thirty minutes Jessica was biting into her pillow, muffling her cries as she climaxed. The sight of her bouncing ass slapping against him made his head spin, a loud rough grunt escaped him as he burst inside of her deliberately. She shuddered as he removed his thick member from inside of her; he collapsed back onto the bed, catching his breath awhile. When he found the strength to move, he threw the covers off and strutted naked to the kitchen and plucked two bottles of water from the refridgerator.

He handed one to Jessica. She sat up, taking sips of water before she corked the bottle and handed it back to Trey.

"Shit. That was awesome," he blurted out.

Trey began stroking his manhood. With one swoop of his free hand he laid Jessica flat on her back and plunged deep inside of her again, his massive shaft expanding and contracting as he darted in and out her. "Ohh baby, don't stop." Jessica's soft moans excited Trey, maddening him and he slammed into her faster and faster. Trey hissed, as he climaxed, his sweat dripping on her naked breasts, he then eased out of her and rolled onto the bed.

"That was so good. Shit," she said.

He smacked her behind as she turned on her stomach. He laid spread eagled on the bed breathing heavy and squeezed his shaft expelling the remainder of his cum. He grabbed a towel and washed his body off in the shower and returned to the bed. Jessica followed suit but when she returned Trey was fast asleep, she sighed. She dressed in a big t-shirt and decided to find a good movie to watch. Annoyed, she watched tv while Trey slept. She wanted a snack, so she popped a large bowl of popcorn and ate and watched tv until she felt sleepy. Crunching and eating, she had watched three movies by the time 10:00 p.m. rolled around.

Trey eventually woke up and flipped the channel to sports. She was not interested in watching sports, instead, she picked up her laptop to do a little online shopping; she needed new bikinis and vacation wear. Jessica spent close to $600.00 online; she bought dresses, bikinis, hats and jewelry. They were to arrive well before her trip.

13

Jessica got up early the morning of her and Trey's trip to Cabo. She double checked her suitcase, just to be certain that she had everything, she checked her list and ticked off her passport, laptop, money, credit cards, perfume, undies, deodorant and sanitary supplies, just in case, into her luggage.

Their flight was at 3:00 p.m., she had convinced Charmaine to pick her and Trey up at 1:00 p.m. Jessica had reassigned her work assignments to her colleagues since she would be out of the country, she would still travel with her laptop in the event there was an emergency.

She sent a text to Trey reminding him to pack his passport.

Jessica continued double checking and ticking off her necessities as she went along. Too excited to eat a meal, she made a peanut butter and jelly sandwich, she finished her snack and resumed what she was doing. Jessica showered and started getting ready; she did her famous high bun, slicked her edges and put her hoops in her ears.

Trey came over just as she was dressing. She ran to the door in her undies to open the door, before she could run back to her bedroom, he swooped her up and kissed her, she stopped fussing and melted into his tight embrace before she pushed him away, breathless.

"Charmaine is gonna be here soon."

"Ok fine. We have a whole week ahead," he smacked her on her butt when she dashed off.

Following her back to her room, he gathered her luggage and started lining them up by the door. Jessica dressed in a frilly pink and blue wrap dress that ended just above her knees, hugging her body snugly. It was designed with a plunging neckline and gave a good eye to her perky breasts.

Trey ran one single finger down the opening of her dress and she smacked his finger away, shaking her head.

Trey laughed.

Charmaine arrived and they headed to the door.

As Trey approached with the luggage, Charmaine got out and opened the trunk. They chatted idly while Jessica locked her front door. Jessica tossed her purse in the front seat and greeted her sister, they all piled into the car and headed to the airport.

Traffic was light for a Friday afternoon, especially on the highway. Charmaine pulled into the designated drop off area and Jessica and Trey exited the car. Charmaine stepped out and wished them a safe trip. Jessica handed Charmaine her house keys and hugged and thanked her for helping her out. She slung her purse over her shoulder and helped Trey with the luggage.

They checked in and took seats in the waiting area.

As she sat scanning the faces of the other travellers, she recognized a few people. She acknowledged those she made eye contact with a slight nod of her head.

Her eyes grazed over a handsome man dressed casually, sitting next to a woman dressed equally as casual. They were sitting four rows across from where she and Trey sat, she vaguely recognized the woman. She looked at the man, doing a double take, Jessica nearly broke her neck. It was Ron. Ron and Lydia. His ex-wife.

Of all the got damn places, she thought.

She couldn't believe it. She did not see the children. They were probably going on vacation alone.

He was looking directly at her. Jessica shifted slightly in her seat, she immediately felt trapped and uncomfortable.

He was still looking at her.

"I'm going to the drink machine, you want anything?" he asked, standing.

"No. I'm fine."

Trey went over to the machine, but there were three people ahead of him.

Jessica pulled out her phone, trying to ignore the stares from across the crowded airport. She angled her neck to see if Trey was at the machine. He was next in line.

A flight was called and the travellers sitting in the rows directly in front of her left and those were now empty.

Jessica felt like a deer in headlights. She felt naked and unprotected.

Why wouldn't he stop staring at her, dammit.

When another flight was called, the travellers seated

across from her on Ron's side began to leave their seats. Ron could now see her clearly. His ex was speaking animatedly, making subtle gestures with her hands.

Jessica took her chapstick out and applied a generous amount on her lips, she returned it to her bag and looked straight ahead. She frowned at him. He lowered his head and chuckled, an act that did not go unnoticed by his ex-wife.

Lydia was now also staring at Jessica. She turned to her husband and whispered something in his ears.

Great.

Thankfully, her flight was announced. Both she and Trey stood and gathered their luggage, Trey gently caressed her lower back as she bent to pull the handle of her suitcase upright.

She could feel their eyes piercing the back of her head. She took one final glance back at them. Both Ron and Lydia were staring at her.

14

The view from the sky was amazing. Being so close to the clouds was so euphoric. Seven hours later they were in Mexico. They collected their luggage from the carousel and caught a taxi to their Resort hotel. Jessica felt extremely happy, she cupped Trey's hand in hers as she took in the sights while the driver flew down the highway. The drive from the airport took about twenty minutes and she could eventually see the hotel from the highway, it was a huge building, made entirely of glass and stone, the sign etched on a stone block said 'The Cape'.

Trey took care of paying the taxi driver while Jessica stood taking in this piece of glorious architecture. He unpacked the trunk and placed their luggage on the concrete path. Entering the Resort, they were both in awe; the marble floors, the huge chandeliers, the beautiful water fountain and the flashing iridescent lights. There was a bar opposite the reception area and a beautiful encased fish tank below the reception desk, everything was sparkling and glam. Both of them had seen gorgeous hotels before but this was outstanding.

They spent thirty minutes checking in and the bell boy soon came and packed their luggage onto the trolley and led them to the elevators.

Their hotel room was equally as gorgeous as the reception area. A big canopy bed sprinkled with red rose petals were nestled in the center of the bed. Just off of the entrance to the balcony was a small indoor pool fit for a party of two. Stepping out bare feet onto the balcony, they could see the vast coastline and the ocean, their suite was so high up that the gigantic resort pool and deck chairs looked miniature.

Jessica returned from the balcony and continued touring the expansive suite. The bell boy was gone by then. Trey circled her, he spun her around, her dress slipping open and he reached beneath her dress, palming her ample behind.

"Not yet," she forced his hand from beneath her dress.

"Uhhh"

"Let's order some food and chill for a moment."

Jessica asked him to order room service while she freshened up.

She changed from her frilly dress to a green shorts pants set she bought from Fashion Nova.

After she was finished, Trey washed up as well. He had changed to a vest and blue cargo shorts.

Since they were there for the week, she set her cosmetics and toiletries in the bathroom vanity. While they waited for room service, they turned the tv on and snuggled on the bed.

"I'm so happy, it's been so long since I've said those words," she blushed.

"I'm happy too." I've never had so much in common with anyone.

"I love you" Jessica said suddenly.

"I love you too."

"Wanna get married?" he grinned at her.

"Just say the word," she laughed heartily.

There was a knock on the door. Room Service had arrived and they sat on the patio watching the setting sun while nibbling on shrimp tacos, fries, beer and cherry soda.

After the sun had gone down, they took the party inside. Trey went to his suitcase and brought back a deck of cards.

"Strip poker?" he asked shaking the stack at her.

"Shooottt, it's over for you now!" she said snapping her fingers.

Jessica was beating Trey unmercifully, five games in and he was butt naked. He slid right next to Jessica, pressing his rock hard manhood into her thigh.

Jessica clasp her fingers around his stiffness and she rhythmically began stroking her hand up and down. Trey's moans soon became louder and his heavy breathing increased. She continued stroking him up and down, his pelvis bucking against her hand. Ten minutes later, he came in rapid bursts, shooting his cum, that ran slowly down her hand, she didn't stop until he had ejected all of his load, she left him on the bed panting and went into the bathroom to rinse her hands, she grabbed a few wipes and returned to him. She cleaned him off and tossed the used wipes into the trash bin in the corner.

Trey pulled her unto him and kissed her intensely. They spent the rest of the evening entangled on the patio watching the waves crash onto the shore.

Breakfast arrived around 8:00 a.m., the next day. They wanted to spend a few hours lounging by the pool so she asked Trey to go down and secure them two lounge chairs allowing her time to get ready.

Jessica chose a sexy, strappy gold bikini that stuck to her body like glue. It had a liquid gold effect; it amplified her flat tummy and ample behind. She adjusted the bikini around her crotch area, she wasn't about to flash strangers, she wasn't that type of girl. She fluffed her natural hair out, applied mascara to her lashes and natural lip gloss to her lips and added her hoop earrings to complete her look. From the moment Jessica hit the pool, all eyes were on her, as she walked, the bikini started to slide further into her butt. She stopped mid stride, searching the deck for Trey. Trey was sitting in the swim-up bar chatting with the bartender, who by now was no longer listening to him, he swiveled his head to see what had taken the Bartender's attention.

Wading through the water, was Jessica approaching them. She was a vision in her liquid gold bikini, floppy hat and sunglasses, she hopped up onto the bar stool and said hello to the Bartender.

He just stared at her, smiled and asked her "What would you like?"

"Sex on the Beach, strong, thanks."

"I'm gonna bleep bleep the hell out of you when we get back to the room. No doubt," he said bashfully.

"You have zero chill, don't you." Jessica sucked her teeth.

"This view is gorgeous," she said mostly to herself.

They spent at least an hour at the pool bar, drinking and chatting with the Bartender. They thanked the bartender, tipped him and swam out into the open pool. The pool was full, mostly with couples doing what couples do.

Jessica swam up to Trey and placed her arms loosely around his neck. He pulled her into him and she wrapped her legs around his butt. They spoke excitedly about any and everything, they kissed ever so often and he constantly palmed her butt beneath the water. Tired, they left the pool and sat in the lounge chairs. A waitress came and offered them more drinks and food, since they enjoyed the nachos last night, they reordered the same food.

After they dined on more nachos, they went back to the room, showered and decided to go to the Casino located in the hotel.

Trey won one game and Jessica won zero. He showed her how to play Roulette and Black Jack, which she thoroughly enjoyed. They were having a fantastic time together; they laughed and held hands while strolling the huge casino. The games were enticing, emphasized by the pretty display lights. They ended up sitting at the bar close to the entrance of the hotel where they drank a few more drinks before calling it a night.

It was a long day and Jessica was tired. No, she was drunk. Jessica walked directly into the bathroom, she washed her face and brushed her teeth and told Trey she was going to take a nap and probably take in a movie with him later. Jessica was asleep before her head hit the pillow.

15

For the next four days, Jessica and Trey visited a number of tourist attractions; they toured the National Anthropology Museum and The Palace of Fine Arts and ate at various top rated restaurants, they visited the mall and purchased gifts for their family and friends, Jessica was overjoyed to find a heart shaped diamond encrusted bracelet in one of the mall outlets, she purchased one for her and one for Charmaine. Later that afternoon, they walked the beach hand in hand, fingers interlaced together. Trey's arm rested comfortably around her shoulder and her arm around his waist. They decided to stop and watch the sun set. She hugged him, kissing him deeply and earnestly.

"I love you," she said warmly.

"I love you too Mrs. Sommers," he said hugging her tightly. She nuzzled her head beneath the warmth of his neck, Jessica never felt more in love, she caught herself thanking God for sending her a man like Trey. Back at the hotel, she made a reservation for dinner for 7:00 p.m. in the Resort's formal dining hall; she chose to wear a breezy floral summer dress and heels which she hung in the closet.

Dinner was amazing. Sitting across from Trey made her wonder if he was the one. He truly made her happy and she would gladly marry him if he proposed. By the time they got to bed, they crashed, both had way too much to drink and the only thing they could do was to sleep.

It was the final day of Jessica and Trey's 'baecation' and she wanted to stay in the room and enjoy being together, she ordered them a special breakfast and they relaxed inside until they had to check out. She wanted to make this moment unforgettable for both of them.

Before they were finished with breakfast, Jessica handed Trey a gift box. It was covered in blue velvet and tied with a silver bow. In it, was a Rolex watch, one she picked up from the same store she bought the sparkling bracelet now gracing her wrist.

"What's this?" he said wiping his hands and mouth with a napkin.

"Open it," she gushed.

He shook the box to his ears, then he flipped the top of the box open. His eyes shot open. He was speechless.

"A Roli!?" he asked in shock.

The luxury timepiece was silver, a solid gold stripe lined the centre of its straps, the face of the watch was designed with gold roman numerals encased above a green velvet back ground. He loved it.

"Oh baby! I love it!" He leaned over the table and

kissed her.

"I saw it and thought it would be a perfect gift for you in remembrance of our trip," she gushed.

"Thank you," he was stunned.

"You are welcome."

Trey set the time on the watch and then he put the watch on, thanking her once again. While he played with his luxury gift, Jessica sipped the balance of her coffee, she was extremely happy that he was appreciative of his gift, she placed her cup down and started tidying up the room. She occasionally listened to Trey as he read the leaflet that came with the watch.

"You need to start packing. We don't want to be late to the airport babe."

"Yea, you're right," he began slinging shirts, shorts and slacks into his suitcase. He tucked his sneakers and dress shoes on top of the clothing.

With almost everything packed, they showered and made love beneath the flowing water one last time. They tossed the toothbrushes and soaps away and awaited the taxi to take them to the airport. Jessica texted her arrival time and chided her sister not to be late. Their flight landed well after 9:00 p.m., they cleared customs and walked outside to the pickup zone. Charmaine was there waiting.

"Hey sissy!" she shrieked. "How was your trip?"

"It was amazing!" Jessica replied excitedly.

"Hey Trey, did you have a good time?"

"Yip. It was pretty damn good," he replied, smiling.

Trey again, packed the luggage in the trunk while Charmaine and Jessica caught up. What couldn't fit was placed in the back of the car.

They bundled into the car, Jessica sat upfront with Charmaine with Trey and the extra luggage crammed into the back seat. Jessica looked back at him and smiled. He looked extremely uncomfortable.

Charmaine caught Jessica up on all the latest gossip while she was away on vacation.

"Oh damn that's messed up," Jessica blurted out upon hearing that one of her sisters lost $5,000.00 in a Blessing Circle.

"Does Freddy know?" Jessica asked. Freddy was Ashley's husband of four years.

"Hell No," They both busted out laughing at the same time.

Charmaine parked on the curb outside of Jessica's home. They chatted for a while as Jessica gave her snippets of her trip.

"I love him. He's so genuine; he's caring, he's helpful, he treats me right. It's what I've always wanted," tears formed in her eyes, not from sadness but immense happiness.

Charmaine hugged her sister tenderly, gliding her hands up and down her back.

Trey removed the luggage, closed the trunk and joined Charmaine and Jessica by the hood of the car.

He gave a short version of his experience in Mexico and thanked her for picking them up from the airport. They scheduled a date night with Charmaine and her husband.

Jessica settled in at home while Trey took Max for a walk, and to handle some work related business of his own.

Jessica undressed and took a quick shower before opening her laptop, she forgot all about work while she was away. In any event if there was an emergency, someone would have called her cell if she was unreachable via email.

Shit, she thought, her email inbox was full. That meant she had to buckle down tonight and clear her backlog. She poured herself a glass of wine and began clearing her emails, some hours later; she was only 1/3 through. Feeling exhausted, she stood and stretched and poured another glass of wine and went to the couch. She found the remote and found a pretty interesting documentary on the late Maya Angelou, a renowned American poet.

Five minutes in, Trey came over.

He'd taken Max on his walk, fed him and played a game of fetch with him.

She offered him a glass of wine and continued watching the documentary.

She stretched her legs over him and he played with the strings of her shorts.

Hearing a sudden noise behind her, she swung her neck in Trey's direction, he was fast asleep. She spread the throw from the couch over his shoulders and watched the documentary to the end while she worked.

16

Jessica received an invitation to attend a surprise birthday celebration for Charmaine to be held in one month. Strange. Charmaine was not into celebrating her birthday at all and her husband knew that. But, since it was a surprise she could not ask Charmaine about it. The dress code was noted as elegant.

She made a note of the event in her calendar and a mental note to find the perfect dress for the occasion.

Jessica and Trey were now inseparable. He had practically moved in...really it was he and Max and to make the transition easier, she made a few alterations to her home, making space for Trey and Max.

She eventually grew to love Max but she'd never get used to him jumping on her whenever he felt like it.

Jessica visited her parents one evening, after a

showing, she drove out to meet them for dinner. Her dad was concerned that she was working too hard; she reminded him that she loved her job, it was hard work but she loved it. It was her passion.

Her dad also queried her love life. It felt like an interrogation really. They had met Trey maybe three times; her birthday dinner, a small get together at her home and another at her father's Lifetime Achievement Award for his invaluable contribution to Social Work. She told him how much she loved Trey; she was blushing so hard her face was red, she often dreamt of marrying him one day and she let both of her parents know that they spent most of their free time together, she was committed to him and he to her. Jessica believed that he was the one.

"Be careful, that's all I'm saying," her dad stated.

"I am daddy."

Jessica was ready to return home to her man. Talking to her father about Trey made her miss him even more.

She kissed her mum goodbye and her dad walked her to her car.

"I want you to be happy, I mean...after....you know."

"I know daddy. He takes great care of me," she smiled.

"Travel safely," he pecked her on the forehead and opened her car door for her.

She stepped in and waved goodbye.

At the junction, she looked through her rearview mirror and saw her dad still standing in his driveway watching her. She knew he wasn't going to move until she was out of sight.

She smiled at the thought.

The surprise party for Charmaine was the following

Sunday. She forgot to ask her parents what they thought of the surprise party, knowing Charmaine hated celebrating her birthday. She'd just have to wait and see. She worked tirelessly through the week, the only thing propelling her was the shameful excitement she felt from the upcoming drama she was sure to see on Sunday.

On Saturday, she pulled a cute yellow jumpsuit from her closet. It was another deep V number that was sexy yet modest. She washed and flat ironed her hair, so that it would be manageable to style the next day. Then, she made lunch for her and Trey and they took Max for a walk for a little exercise before the sun set.

Sunday Morning, Trey returned to his home after breakfast. Jessica spent most of the day relaxing; she watched tv, surfed the net browsing Instagram and other social media sites and caught up on celebrity gossip; she screamed with delight at some of the insane things some of her faves were up too.

Jessica ate Sunday lunch with Trey at his home and they chatted about the dinner they'd soon be going to.

"What are you wearing," she asked.

"I don't know yet. Something nice I guess."

Jessica cleaned up the kitchen, rubbed Max's head and went home.

As soon as she got home, she set her alarm so that she wouldn't oversleep. She took a nap, sleeping flat on her stomach. The alarm sounded just as Jessica was stirring, she stretched her hand out and hit the snooze button.

She rolled over and sat up.

Throwing the covers off, she slipped out of her short tube top dress and stepped into the shower, she adjusted the hot water setting, lathered and scrubbed her body vigorously before rinsing off, she took her towel off the rack and patted her skin dry. Jessica sat at her vanity and applied her makeup, lashes and mascara, she opted for a bright red lippie; red lipstick made her teeth look extra white when she smiled.

She sneakily called her sister to see what she was up too. Charmaine said her husband had made reservations for dinner at a very exclusive restaurant and she was getting ready; she would chat with Jessica the next day. Jessica propped her phone on a perfume bottle while watching YouTube videos while she added small studded earrings in her ears with the matching necklace.

She checked her hair and makeup once more and then walked over to the mirror and got dressed, she slipped on a pair of nude thong panties and made sure her boobs were taped securely, she'd forgotten how deep the "V" actually was. She slid her hand over her curves and made one turn in the mirror, she flexed her butt muscles in the mirror watching her booty jump and wiggle, she snickered. Pleased that there were no nip slips, she grabbed her purse, and headed downstairs.

She met Trey at the door.

"Damn, you look good baby," he said.

"Thank you, hunny," Jessica was geeked.

She loved when he complimented her. He smacked her on the butt as she was locking her door and she smacked his hand away playfully.

"Later. Maybe," she said jokingly.

Driving up to the venue, Jessica was in awe. The building was decorated with colourful lights that casted different colours on the building, they seemed to be set four feet apart. Jessica loved the pretty lights. It felt like Christmas.

Parking was located on an enormous pasture

opposite the venue.

Trey approached her, breaking her concentration, he took her hand in his and walked her across the gravel to the steps of the building.

There was a beautifully decorated archway at the entrance of the venue, yellow flowers, red roses and bright stringed lights snaked from one end of the archway to the other. No one else was outside. She didn't see any familiar vehicles parked on the pasture and she was sure she'd arrived before her sister and Brother-in-Law. Where were her family members and other guests? She was sure to see folks mingling about.

Inside was much more breathtaking.

The foyer was immaculate; big columns, marble floors and gorgeous portraits made the space look enchanting.

They rounded the corner off of the foyer. It was dark, that's weird.

"Are we supposed to be...?" she started to say.

Suddenly, bright lights pierced her eyes.

"SURPRISEEEEE," everyone screamed.

17

Jessica was confused.

Why were they screaming 'surprise' at them, she looked dumbfounded. Charmaine and her husband were there already. What the hell was happening? She saw her parents, both were crying. Her sisters, crying; Charmaine was boo hooing loud as hell. Her boss? Huh?

Jessica noticed Trey was no longer next to her. She turned around. Trey was behind her, on his knees, smiling from ear to ear and she could see all of his teeth. In his hand was a similar gift box to the box she gifted him. She still didn't understand. It took her a moment before she finally got it.

Tears rushed to her eyes. She took shaky steps towards him with her family cheering her on, she looked back at them and all of the females were crying.

"Trey..." she couldn't speak. She wanted to cry, her hands flew to her mouth to keep the cries in.

He took a breath and took her left hand. "Jessica Clarke, will you marry me?" His eyes were glassy and clear.

"Yes. Yes I will marry you," she felt weak and slightly lightheaded.

They were immersed in deafening cheers and applause. Trey stood and snatched his fiancé into his arms; they shared a loving kiss but were broken apart by their individual family and friends. Jessica's sisters swooned over the ring. It was an eighteen karat gold ring. It was stunning.

As the engagement party moved into full swing, the newly engaged couple mingled with their guests. Everyone wished them years of wedded bliss, prosperity and good health, wealth and lots of children.

The night was spectacular. The guests danced, sang and drank. It was a night she'd never forget. Trey's parents and brother were in attendance, he introduced Jessica to his fraternity brothers and friends she had never met before. Jessica and Trey were hugged up all night, her dad toasted to them and she hugged and thanked him.

The dinner table was an enthusiastic scene of hi-fives, photo taking and constant chatter. After dinner, her parents were preparing to leave, they argued that they were old and grew tired quickly.

Trey thanked them for coming and walked them to the exit. Jessica asked one of her uncles to bring up her parents car, and as they waited outside, her mum told her how happy she was for her, she hugged her mum and nodded, she was too emotional to respond. When Uncle Luke pulled up, she helped her mum into her seat and closed the door and waited for her dad to drive off. When the car was out of sight, she returned inside to her fiancé.

Trey was also ready to get his fiancé home; they had spent four hours partying. He signaled for everyone's attention; he thanked them for coming and for sharing in the beginning of an amazing love story. He ended by saying "You don't have to go home but you have to get the hell out of here." Everyone laughed hysterically.

Making it home safely, they crashed on the bedroom floor.

Jessica was overwhelmed. She was getting married. Could it be this easy?

Trey spoke up.

"Penny for your thoughts?" he squeezed her hand gently.

"Aww man, tonight was so amazing," she said wiping away fallen tears. "Seeing everyone there; happy just to see me happy."

She sat up on resting on her elbows, facing him, "When did you buy the ring?"

"At the same jewelry store where you bought me the watch," he said wickedly.

She laughed. "I didn't see you checking out any rings."

"Remember I was looking for a gift for my mum, I secretly asked the guy to bring me something spectacular," he said grinning like a Cheshire cat.

"Hmmm," she paused. "Thank you."

"Thank me for what?" he asked, frown lines adorning his face.

"For loving me for me, for seeing a future with me," she cried.

"This might sound cliché, but, I loved you from the first moment I saw you."

Jessica made a noise with her mouth.

"I was outside playing around with Max. You drove up, got out your car and stopped by your mailbox. I was like damn, son, shorty is fine. You went inside and came back out because I guess you forgot something in your car, I kept seeing you whenever I was out with Max, so I made it a priority to meet you and I did," he continued, "The more time we chilled together, the more it was confirmed for me that I liked the person you were."

"Awwww," Jessica sing-songed.

"I would sometimes get lost just staring at you, the way you ate; the way you held your fork or the way you would look at me when we were talking, with those pretty brown eyes. You were hypnotic."

"Let's go to bed," she said seductively.

Trey unzipped her outfit and dropped her panties to the floor, she turned and helped him out of his clothes, they laid beneath the covers and snuggled together. Once more, as the night turned into day, Jessica found herself staring at the ceiling with Trey's face hidden between her legs, she closed her eyes and enjoyed the intimate sounds emitting from below her waist. They made love well into the late morning.

As she prepared breakfast later in the afternoon, she couldn't stop thinking about her engagement party. She was completely surprised. Her parents being there; she remembered thinking her dad was interrogating her when he asked her about Trey and their relationship, now she understood why. She chuckled "Daddy, daddy, daddy," she said. Did Trey asked her dad for her hand in marriage? She wondered. She would have to ask him when she saw him.

Jessica and Charmaine were in full wedding mode.

The wedding was in less than five months, the week before Christmas.

Jessica had hired a fantastic wedding planner, she

was referred to by one of her colleagues, they swapped photos of venues and floral arrangements intermittently and she was also supplied with a wide selection of food suggestions to choose from. The hardest part for Jessica was the seating. Who sits next to whom?

She was also on the hunt for the perfect wedding dress. She made appointments with several dress shops and hoped that one of them had what she needed. Jessica's first dress fitting was a success; she found a stunning backless white mermaid styled lace dress. The fit was incredible. The bustier top thrust her breasts up and the slim design of the waist made her appear even curvier than she was. Not bad. Her sisters thought this was the one. They had made it abundantly clear that they had to be at every fitting.

Her sisters were also her Bridesmaids and they needed to be fitted as well, by the second and third dress fittings, Jessica was extremely annoyed; one sister liked one dress and the other hated it. It was total confusion.

"Ok one more dress and then I'm done," she was upset and they knew it.

Her next bridal dress was designed with a sweetheart neck and a can-can bottom, another beautiful fit but not for her.

"This is gorge, boo," Rebecca piped up.

"You look like a princess," offered Olivia.

Charmaine remained mute; she knew Jessica would never pick that dress.

"It's not YOU," Charmaine acknowledged.

Jessica returned to the changing room.

As the sisters drank Champagne, Ashley said "I saw Ron at the gym the other day," she looked back to see if Jessica was in earshot, "he wanted to know whether it was true that Jess was getting married."

"What did you say?" Rebecca asked.

"I told him yes, to a wonderful man. I wanted to cuss his ass out, but I was out in public. He has some balls," she said incredulously.

"Please don't mention any of that to her," Charmaine said.

Jessica returned, dressed in her civilian clothes, they decided to go to lunch at a quaint restaurant across the street.

They piled in around a table with a seating for five and asked the waitress for the menus. Jessica was not entirely hungry but she ordered a chicken Caesar salad anyway.

"Have you decided on the menu yet?" Alexus asked.

"I'm waiting on Trey. I know what I want already," Jessica said.

"What's taking him so long?" Olivia persisted.

"Hell if I know," she said.

"Just make sure there's some good old fashioned fried chicken," Rebecca joined in. They all snickered behind their menus.

"Are you gonna have a second dress for the reception?" Charmaine asked.

"Yip, I've ordered it already," she took her phone from her coat pocket and pulled up the pic of her reception ensemble.

It was a sleek white lace jumpsuit, its long sleeves made of an intricate lace design, its bodice covered in Swarovski crystals.

"That's hot," Charmaine said.

"It is," They all said in unison.

"Damn girl, you are gonna look fire. I love it," Olivia said.

"That's right, bitchesssss," Jessica sing-songed.

That all clinked their glasses together, laughing.

The ladies ate and drank, recalling moments from their childhood; from awards to beatings, swimming lessons to boys, marriage and babies.

"Does Trey want kids right away?" Rebecca asked.

"Yes. Not right away though. I want to enjoy our first year together. No babies please," Jessica replied.

"I don't blame you," Ashley chimed in, "Kids are stress and a ton of money," she continued.

"Money isn't a problem for us," Jessica stated.

"Cheers to that," Alexus said.

"My advice to you is to have your own savings account, there's nothing wrong with a joint account for the bills etc. Never join your money so soon," Olivia countered.

"I have to agree with you there O," Ashley stated.

"That's true to some extent, but, YOU have to decide the best method for you and Trey," Charmaine added.

They shared another round of drinks before going their separate ways.

Jessica thanked her sisters for their unwavering support, even when she was being a brat. They kissed and hugged goodbye and left Jessica to settle the bill.

"Thanks you guys," she said sarcastically handing the waitress her Visa Card as her sisters exited.

Jessica replaced her card in her wallet and met the others outside.

"I saw Ron at the gym and he asked me if the rumours were true of you getting married," Alexus rattled off quickly before Charmaine could knock her head off.

"I hope you told him to fuck off," Jessica replied.

"Nope. I praised Trey for being an awesome man and how in love and happy you are," she beamed.

They all laughed and hi-fived each other.

They said their second round of goodbyes and Jessica made a quick stop at the gas station before going home.

18

With the wedding day fast approaching, Jessica insisted that Trey get fitted for his tux before he took a short business trip. She did not want any surprises. All the necessary arrangements were in place; the venue, the food, her wedding dress and her sisters' dresses and accessories. She also made an appointment with an artist to cover her hair and makeup.

The honeymoon trip would be another surprise. It was their wedding gift from her parents. They would only find out where they were going after the nuptials.

She was excited. She hoped it was somewhere exotic.

By late November, Jessica decided to put up and decorate her Christmas tree. She took her decorations and ornaments from the garage and set up the tree in her patio. She put Max in his crate; he kept running off with the Christmas balls. She got the tree up and added red and gold decorations and strung the lights and big bows around the tree. She flipped the Christmas lights on and took photos of her tree. After that, she took her boxes inside and placed a few décor pieces on the ledge of the fire place and around her home and added a Christmas reef on the outside of her front door.

Trey came home that Saturday evening from his trip.

He asked her to join him on a walk with him and Max.

"How do you feel?" Max was tugging and pulling against his leash.

"I'm a little tired. I just want the day to occur without a single hitch," she said.

"Anything I can do to help?" he was concerned. "You can't burn yourself out, or make yourself sick."

"Thankfully, all the arrangements are in place so I'll be able to relax from now on."

They walked to the park and allowed Max to run and roam freely until Jessica started feeling cold and wanted to return home.

She stretched out lazily on the couch and he brought her a bowl of fruit; strawberries, grapes and kiwi, her favourite. She thanked him and started munching on kiwi first.

"How about a scary movie?" he asked enthusiastically.

"Nope," Jessica replied, "Then I can't sleep tonight. No thanks."

"Then what do you feel like watching?"

"A comedy!"

Trey looked at her dubiously.

Jessica cracked up laughing.

"We could take this party upstairs," he moved his hand beneath her top groping her breasts.

Max came bounding up on the couch. He laid his head on Jessica's leg.

"Thanks Max," she ruffled his mane.

Trey sucked his teeth and laid back on the couch, very annoyed.

Jessica played a little more with Max to the further annoyance of Trey.

"Are you really gonna ignore me Jess?" he said.

"I'm not ignoring you, just choose the movie." She was still playing with Max.

Trey got up and flung the remote onto the couch and stormed out to the patio.

Jessica stopped rubbing Max's head and followed him, pausing slightly by the patio door before proceeding to sit opposite him on the patio.

"I'm not ignoring you." Trey was looking straight ahead. He didn't acknowledge her.

"I just got back home from my trip, and it's like you didn't even miss me. No hug. No kiss. Nothing."

"I'm sorry. I wasn't trying to hurt your feelings, I did miss you and I am happy you are home," she said soothingly.

She kissed him on his cheek.

"I love you. I'd never hurt you willingly."

He took her hand and kissed her fingertips, he then discreetly placed her hand over his swollen bulge. She felt a sudden throb between her legs, she kissed him slowly, he wanted her so badly he felt like he was trying to eat her face. She slyly unzipped Trey's jeans and then slipped her panties off while he shifted his boxers and jeans around his ankles.

She straddled him. Her breath catching in her throat as she slid all the way down his shaft, she felt her slit expand and contract around his full length. Trey moaned, his warm breath tingling the hairs on her neck. Jessica skillfully bounced up and down on his rock solid rod, slamming down on him repeatedly.

"Don't stop baby," he eagerly grabbed her butt and guided her up and down as she rode him. Swiftly, he slid half his body off of the patio bench with only his shoulders nestled on the edge of the hard surface, Jessica remained seated on top of him and readjusted her legs without missing a beat, she continued driving her slippery slit up and down his swollen shaft, she was literally on her tippy toes, "Spread your legs for me baby," Jessica complied.

Trey rammed into her freely, the slight change of position adding to the depth of his thrusts "Oh FUCK," she cried, he was right there, three powerful thrusts later, his cum was dripping out of her. "Got damn, baby," he growled, squirting even more cum inside of her, they were both breathing hard, after a minute or two Jessica slowly shifted from above him, his jizz dripping down her legs. She took her panties and wiped the cum from between her legs before going to the washroom and grabbing a warm rag for Trey. He cleaned himself off and tossed the rag on the floor. How quaint! She thought.

He pulled his boxers and jeans up and rested his head against the wall of the house and drew Jessica to him.

"I love you," he said sweetly.

"I love you too."

19

The wedding was only days away.

Jessica reconfirmed with her Wedding Planner that everything was in place. She collected her dress and the bridesmaids' dresses for her sisters and delivered them to the venue. They were dressing at the venue so she arranged for the items to be packed and taken to there. Trey was responsible for his tux and his Groomsmen. Their shoes, belts and bowties were also to be delivered to the venue.

She had visited the location to ensure that the décor and seating were arranged as she envisioned. Everything was beautiful, so beautiful that she began to cry. She'd been dreaming of this moment for years. It would be hers in a few hours. To celebrate her upcoming nuptials, Jessica, her sisters and a few close friends, who were also at her birthday dinner decided to hit up a strip club down town for a small bachelorette party. Jessica was elated to finally wear her 'Bride To Be Sash and veil'.

The strip club was packed with females. Male strippers were pillar to post, some of the ladies were gyrating on the strippers and others were tucking dollar bills in their g-strings. It was a mess. They headed to the bar and ordered a round of drinks. The strippers on stage were in tip top shape. They were tough and buff in all the right places. They were there for a private show so they were escorted to the backroom by a very handsome young man in a cute red bowtie and nothing else.

They sat in front of a circular stage with huge curtains hung in the back. Their seats were arranged around the stage. The lights were dimmed and sexy music played in the background. Two male strippers appeared on stage, both hard bodied black men. The lights were raised. These men were gorgeous, their bulging muscles exaggerated by the slick layer of oil covering them. They could have easily hopped out of a body building magazine. The long nosed elephant stockings dangling from their crotches made the ladies squeal with delight. They sure weren't baby elephants.

The music changed to a more up tempo beat as they began their routine.

One of the strippers, started whining his hips as he walked over to Jessica. He took hold of her hands and ran them down his oily chest. He sat in her lap gyrating and rolling his butt and oil all over her. He stood, thrusting his elephant in her flushed face. The atmosphere was frantic. As the music switched again, the stripper removed his elephant stocking. His body was a work of art and was impressive to say the least. He approached Jessica again while his friend worked the floor tantalizing the other ladies, keeping them occupied.

Jessica sat back in her seat, eagerly waiting what was to come next. She took a glance back at the ladies...and as the saying goes, what happens in Vegas stays in Vegas. ☺

By the time she reached home, Trey was fast asleep. She wondered if his bachelor party was as interesting as hers.

The day of her wedding began like any other day, except it was not.

Trey spent the night at his home with his parents and brother, they arrived earlier in the week to attend the wedding.

Jessica had hired a luxury buses to collect them all and take them to the venue. The ladies had their own bus and the men had theirs. When the ladies arrived, they exited the bus and filed into the suite and immediately began unpacking. The ladies' dresses were hung in the closet, each dress was tagged with the respective name and the accessories and shoes were placed below each dress.

The ladies wore robes labeled 'Bridesmaid' and gladly sipped on wine as their hair was styled and makeup applied. As soon as the ladies were finished, Jessica took a seat and with a glass of wine in hand and began her transformation. When the artist was finished, Jessica took a long look at the woman staring back at her in the mirror. Her mind wandered fleetingly to Ron, for a long time she had dreamt of this moment with him.

She was beautiful. Her makeup was exquisite, an

elegant glam look was what she wanted. Her hair was drawn away from her face in a loose bun. Tendrils of curly hair cascaded down to her shoulders from the loose knot of the bun. Charmaine walked over with her dress. Jessica stood, disrobed and placed the dress close to her body as she viewed herself in the standing mirror.

She pulled the zip down and stepped into the dress. This was the moment everyone was waiting for. Jessica had chosen the dress from her first dress fitting. The mermaid styled white dress. She adjusted the strapless bustier top around her breasts and her sister Olivia, clasp the hook at the back. Her curvaceous body was amplified by the snug fit of the dress. She looked fabulous.

"Girllll. You look amazing!" Ashley blurted out.

"Body Body Ody," Charmaine gushed.

The room was silent. Everyone was in awe.

"You look gorgeous Jessica," her makeup artists said.

The Wedding Planner announced that it was thirty minutes until showtime.

There was a burst of activity as the ladies checked and rechecked themselves in the mirrors. Jessica slipped on her jewelry, centering her necklace and slid on her white lace gloves.

"Veil please," Jessica said. She was getting anxious.

Charmaine rushed over with the veil. She assisted with placing it on Jessica's head. "Oh my God, it's really happening," she cried.

"You're gonna make me cry" Jessica said, "Her eyes already misting."

The ladies gathered around in the room holding hands. Rebecca said a short sweet Prayer.

"Father God, we come before you on this day of Jessica and Trey's wedding. We humbly ask that this day be blessed, that their marriage be blessed and long lasting, that love, devotion and honour be at the forefront of their union. Amen."

"Amen." Everyone said in unison.

It was showtime!

Jessica was led down the hallway to the entrance of the ceremony doors. The wedding party consisted of the Bride, the Maid of Honour and the Bridesmaids; Charmaine, Olivia, Rebecca, Alexus and Ashley. The ladies looked beautiful in their red mermaid styled dresses. Jessica realized that they resembled each other in different ways.

Her sisters and their Groomsmen proceeded into the ceremony.

"You look so beautiful honey," her father said beaming with pride.

"Thank you daddy," she said, smiling up at him. She felt like a little girl again, sharing a special moment with her proud father. The wedding procession song began and Charmaine pulled the veil over her sister's face and returned to her spot behind her sister.

The doors opened. Jessica felt faint. She adjusted the bouquet of white roses in her hand and breathed deeply before placing her free arm into her father's. The entire compliment of attendees stood. Jessica heard the whispers, gasps, 'ohhs' and 'ahhs'. Trey was awestruck. He felt like the luckiest man on earth. Jessica stood opposite Trey at the altar, he looked dashing in his red tuxedo jacket and black tailored pants. They were smiling hard at each other. Charmaine fixed the train of Jessica's dress and stepped to the side of the Bridesmaids.

Trey was nervous. He was rocking from side to side. Handsome as ever in his tux. His nervousness made some of the guests chuckle with laughter. The

Reverend began with his formal dialogue proceeded onto the wedding ritual, after which he requested the rings. Trey's brother stepped forward and handed the rings to him. Jessica's heart was racing as Trey recited his wedding vows to her, she was physically trembling.

Trey continued ..."I give this ring as a sign of my love." He slid the ring onto her trembling finger. He whispered to her "It's ok baby," Jessica breathed deeply, no longer able to withhold the tears streaming down her face. She repeated her vows, "I give this ring as a sign of my love." She slid Trey's ring on his finger. She looked at him and he also had tears in his eyes. He took his free hand and wiped his eyes.

The Reverend continued... "You have declared your consent before God; I now pronounce you husband and wife. You may now kiss your bride."

Trey shakily lifted the veil to reveal his beautiful bride's face. He took a few steps towards her and passionately kissed his new wife to the thunderous applause of their guests. Mr. and Mrs. Sommers descended from the podium through the aisle, their first walk as man and wife. Jessica held on tightly to Trey, too afraid she would fall. Her legs felt like jello. Congratulations were shouted at them as they walked through the aisle to the exit followed by the bridal party.

The wedding reception banquet was within walking distance of the ceremony. Jessica returned to her suite, used the restroom and changed from her formal wedding dress to her lace white jumpsuit. She had her makeup touched up while the guests were led to the reception hall awaiting the arrival of her and Trey. She returned to the banquet area where Trey waited on the outside. She smiled as soon as she saw him.

"You look amazing, my beautiful wife."

"Thank you, my handsome husband."

Charmaine was the MC for the night. She did a little housekeeping, indicating to the guests where the washrooms were and she then introduced the newlyweds and the bridal party.

The Dj played Patti Labelle's 'My Love Sweet Love' as the Bride and Groom entered. They arrived into the reception party to more cheers and applause. Big smiles were plastered all over their faces. They posed for a few photos with the photographer before sitting. The bridal party table was stretched at least eight feet long. Jessica and Trey were seated in the centre and the bridal party sat at the opposite ends of them.

Their parents and immediate family were seated at the front of the Bride and Bridegroom's table. They were twenty circular tables, seating ten guests per table. The tables were all adorned with a bouquet of white roses similar to Jessica's, one large lit candle sat discreetly in the centre of each table arrangement. The tables were covered with white table cloths and silver and lace accessories. A few trinkets were scattered loosely on the table as further decor. The cushioned chairs were decorated with a single red velvet bow, tied around the chair backs. The big bows were facing outwards.

20

Charmaine returned to the podium, to announce the toasters to the guests.

Mr. Clarke was honoured to be speaking again on his daughter's behalf. He retold the same stories from her birthday dinner. He ended with "Cherish each other, never go to bed angry and always, always put God first." Jessica was teary eyed again. These were happy tears. She was happy.

"Amen." A few of the guests declared.

Trey approached the podium. "On behalf of my wife and myself...," he began.

The guests all started cheering.

"On behalf of my WIFE and myself, I am truly thankful. Thank you all, our parents and invited guests for celebrating in the biggest and happiest moments in both of our lives. Please eat, mingle and dance and have a wonderful time. Thank you."

They were thunderous howls and bird calls from Trey's college buddies.

Trey's brother Samuel spoke on his behalf. He spoke eloquently and highly of his brother. Being the older sibling, he praised himself on being the person Trey molded himself after. He cracked a few jokes at Trey's expense but he ended thanking Trey for allowing him to be a part of his special occasion. He wished the newlyweds joy, lots of love and success in their marriage.

After the toasts, the banquet table was open.

There were a wide range of dishes; grilled and fried chicken with sweet spring vegetables, lobster mac and cheese, macaronie pie, brisket with mashed potatoes, shrimp and grits, shrimp with jasmine rice and tossed salad. The bridal party and the couple's immediate family were served first. The other guests were called by table number to the banquet table to defer any congestion in the lines.

After dinner, Charmaine introduced the couple to have their 'first dance' as newlyweds. Luther Vandross song 'Here and Now' began floating through the sound system as Trey took his wife's hand and escorted her to the dance floor. He lovingly embraced Jessica and she melted into his arms, he felt so good to her; she felt so loved and protected. He whispered into her ears "I love you."

"I love you too," she said, water springing into her eyes.

They swayed to the music still tightly hugged up on each other, Jessica's arms loosely around his neck and his arms snugly around his waist.

After fifteen minutes, Charmaine took the stage again "Let's hear it for the beautiful couple." The guests broke out in cheers and applause. The dance floor was now open.

The Dj brought the house downnnnn. He played numerous tracks from up-beat to slow jams, rhythm and blues to rock and pop to a little gospel, it created the perfect atmosphere for a night to remember.

Charmaine announced it was time for the bouquet throw.

"Calling all of the single ladies, please line up, let's get you down the aisle next" Charmaine said jokingly.

Ten giggling ladies lined up, each jostling the other in anticipation of the throw. Jessica backed them and raised the bouquet above her head, she flung her hands back and stopped, she was dying with laughter as the ladies almost knocked each other over.

"Aww come on, Jess" one piped up.

"Ok. I'm done. I'm done," she said her stomach knotting from laughter.

She threw the bouquet over her head. There was a mad dash for the bouquet, shrieks, screams and laughter filled the air as the ladies jostled for the prize. Jessica was not sure who won, she was crying laughing.

Charmaine announced the cutting of the cake next. Jessica cleared her eyes, making her way to the table to cut the wedding cake. A three tier vanilla chocolate cake adorned with a beautiful miniature cake topper of the bride and groom that resembled them. The guests ambled over to the table surrounding Jessica and Trey. Trey kissed Jessica on her check. They held the knife together, and sliced the cake together. Jessica offered a piece to Trey, which he delightfully accepted. It was his turn. Trey took a piece of cake on the fork and fed it to Jessica. She slipped it in her mouth and swallowed it whole to the enthusiasm of their guests.

The night ended superbly. The merriment and the joy exuded by their guests for their union was overwhelming. Jessica and Trey went around to each table expressing their gratitude to their family and invited guests in making their wedding a success.

They said their goodbyes to her family and departed the reception, headed to their hotel suite.

Jessica asked Trey to unzip her. He stood behind her and traced his hands along the curves of her body. He kissed her bare shoulders and she instinctively angled her neck to kiss him. His breath was warm and smelled of alcohol. He slipped the rest of her jumper over her ample curves, stopping briefly to fondle her round behind. Their kiss continued, never stopping. Trey undid his belt, his pants falling to the floor. He released his bulging erection as Jessica stepped out of her thong panties. She pressed her hands against the wall as he spread her legs apart, she was dripping wet by the time he entered her. "Damn, you're wet." He gripped her around her waist and thrust deeply into her. Jessica moaned loudly, bracing herself against the vigorous pounding she was receiving. Trey was hammering her from behind for what seemed like eternity. She bit her lip "Shit," she said. She couldn't take anymore, "Trey!" she yelped, her breath fast and choppy. Jessica pressed her arms against the wall, taking all of him as best she could. Trey was in his zone giving her every last inch of himself and she could not escape.

He plunged further and deeper. Jessica grunted. He grabbed one of her breasts. He began pumping her core, harder and faster from behind. Thinking she could bear no more, he finally exploded inside of her. "Fuckkkk," he gasped, the sweat from his face, dripping onto his dress shirt. He leaned his head back sucking in much needed oxygen as he slowly withdrew from her.

Jessica slumped to the floor and stretched out on her back, one hand placed between her legs, the other caressing her breasts. He rubbed her wet pearl with one finger in a circular motion. She quivered as she quickly brought herself to climax. Trey stood looking down at her. The wet, sticky sounds of Jessica's centre made him rock hard again. He stroked his thick member in anticipation of devouring his wife once more. As Jessica's climax subsided, he fell to his knees and anchored one of her legs above his shoulder and glided straight into her silky mound, she clenched her walls around his engorged shaft as he enticed her towards another sweet orgasm. Jessica felt his body jerk and spasm, his cum spilling inside her. Sated, they melted together on the floor, the scent of their lovemaking intoxicating, his head lay between her breasts and he could hear the thumping of her heart in his ears. They stayed there on the floor spent from their lovemaking.

Mindful of her work obligations, Jessica pushed the honeymoon back, luckily they were open tickets. She discussed this with Trey and thankfully, he was very understanding and supported her decision. For the next two days, the newlyweds stayed locked in their hotel suite; they made love, they slept, they ordered room service and soaked in the Jacuzzi.

"Did you call your mum back? Trey asked, "She's probably concerned she hasn't heard you since the wedding."

"Hmm, I will, she will understand that I was a little busy," she winked at Trey seductively.

"As much as we have enjoyed our stay, it's time to go husband," she loved saying that word.

Jessica opened the suitcases and shuffled their clothes and toiletries into them. When they first arrived she returned her wedding dress and veil to its protective clear bag and hung it in the closet, she took the bag from the hook and folded them in half. She placed them at the very top of her suitcase and placed all her jewelry and accessories in the second compartment of her suitcase. She did the same for Trey's tux, shoes and toiletries and placed the suitcases by the front door.

Jessica checked to make sure they left nothing behind. She returned the key to front desk and they headed home.

Trey unloaded her car and pulled both suitcases inside.

The interior of the home was decorated with a Welcome Home banner, balloons and congratulatory cards from invited guests who were unable to attend were neatly arranged on the table.

Jessica began reading the cards aloud. There was a combination of well wishes and congratulations from both of their friends and colleagues.

"So sweet," Jessica sing-songed.

"Yip," Trey agreed.

Trey immediately loaded the washing machine as soon as he unpacked their suitcases, at some point Jessica would take her dress and his tux to the Laundromat.

They sat at the kitchen island drinking coffee, the temperature both inside and outside was chilly; it was always chilly around December. Jessica sighed, she was totally exhausted; she'd hardly slept in five days.

Trey placed her leg on his thigh and rubbed her feet.

"That feels sooo good."

He rubbed and kneaded her feet for another 15 minutes.

They eventually switched to the living room and

Trey turned the tv on. "I wanna catch the game," he said.

"Fine. I've got some work to do anyway." She thought of going into her office but thought better of it, she seldom used the office anymore.

Jessica set up her laptop, signing into her Gmail account. She scanned her emails, responding to those that requested urgent replies. The others would have to wait until she returned to work.

"When will the tenants be moving in?" he asked, his eyes not leaving the game.

"Early in the new year," she stated.

Trey did not want to sell his home, instead he asked Jessica to place it for rent on the market. She soon received a hit and those tenants would be moving in soon.

21

Christmas dinner was to be held this year at Jessica's parents' home outside of the City.

The day before the dinner, she ran to the mall to pick up a few items. She stopped at Salt's bakery and bought a fruit cake and a bouquet of red roses for her mum. The stores were closing early so she was in a rush to get her shopping done early and avoid last minute shoppers. Besides, she and Trey wanted to have an intimate dinner in the evening where they would exchange their gifts.

Jessica and Trey set out around 9:00 a.m. on Christmas morning en route to her parents. They called his mother before they set off to wish her and Samuel, Merry Christmas.

They were the first to arrive. They wished her

JESSICA

parents Merry Christmas. She handed the cake and roses to her mum and they went off to the kitchen. She started setting the table as her husband and dad sat playing a raucous game of chess.

Her sisters and their partners along with their children arrived shortly after. As the older ladies prepped and cooked in the kitchen, Jessica and Olivia huddled by the faux fire place enjoying the dancing fake flames.

"Soo, how do you like married life?" she asked.

"It's great. I love it. I have zero complaints," she said snickering.

"How's he in bed?" she said interestingly.

"It's the same as it was." Jessica said breaking out laughing. "Was it to the change sis?"

"How was the wedding night?"

"Girl, what the hell is wrong with you?" They were rolling on the floor cracking up.

"What's so funny?" her mother asked, walking by.

"Nothing," they said straight faced.

By 1:30 p.m. they were seated to a feast.

The Christmas menu consisted of baked ham, fried chicken, jasmine rice, shrimp, corn bread, jug jug, cole slaw and salad.

The wine list was just as extensive; vodka, champagne and red and white wine. Jessica had two glasses of white wine before dinner was served. She downed a third glass and then dived into her packed plate. While the dishes were passed from person to person, the conversation turned to the weeding and how amazing it was and what a gorgeous couple Jessica and Trey made; politics, their jobs, and everything under the sun were discussed intermittently.

The children sat at a separate table eating and watching tv, children were always separated from the adults, there was no telling when the conversation

130

would turn salacious.

After dinner, Jessica sliced the fruit cake into sections and served them around the table. The gents moved to the patio with the rum while the ladies washed the dishes and cleared the table. Take away containers were filled, leaving enough for mum and dad for the next two days.

After washing the dishes and tidying the kitchen, the ladies all gathered in the living room. The Christmas cd was playing sweetly from the stereo. The Christmas lights were dancing and flashing green, red and blue intricately against the walls. The sisters played a game of spades and uno while ignoring the boisterous voices of the men that invaded the living room space. By 10:00 p.m. Jessica was sleepy. She signaled to Trey that she was ready to go. Before she left, her mum handed her the envelope containing the plane tickets to her and Trey's honeymoon destination. She thanked her mum and headed to put on her coat. They said their goodbyes to the others and headed home. They were many homes decorated with snowmen and twinkling lights along the route to the highway, they were so pretty, she thought. She loved Christmas.

Jessica returned to work the second week of January. A meeting was called as soon as she entered the building. It took an hour and a half before she was able to get back to her desk. She scheduled a few meetings with clients that she might have neglected leading up to her wedding.

She opened her laptop and signed in to her Gmail account. Her cell started ringing and she immediately put it to her ear again without looking at the caller ID.

"Jessica Sommers, Good Morning."

"Hey. It's me. Ron."

Jessica was silent. Shock coursed through her entire body.

"Congratulations on your wedding," he said glumly.

"What do you want Ron?"

"I only wanted to offer you congratulations on your marriage."

"You did that. Look, I'm busy and I don't want to play catch up with you," she said sternly. "We aren't cool like that, ok?"

"Jess, wait. I need to speak with you. The investment properties you hooked me up with I would like to sell those and set that money aside for my kids. Would you be able to handle it?"

"Ron, you can take those to any other Agent you desire and have them put those on the market for you."

"I want you to handle them personally."

"I can't."

"Why? This is business, I'm not trying to play games with you. I want to sell those homes now that the market is good."

"You know why," she countered.

"Can we meet to discuss this in person? Can you meet me at home on 4th   Avenue?"

"I am not meeting you at home," she said taken aback.

"What are you afraid off? I'm not gonna hurt you."

"Fine. 5:00 p.m. today. Bye." She ended the call. She leaned back in her chair, twirling a pen between her fingers, unease running through her.

Jessica pulled up her reports and began editing them. She left the office at 1:00 p.m. and met with a few clients throughout the day. She grabbed lunch and decided to eat in her car. Her final appointment was at

3:00 p.m., that would give her enough time to get to Ron's. She ate while preparing her notes for her meeting. An hour later, she was headed to Ron's Condo on 4th Avenue. She parked in the driveway, sitting and contemplating. She wanted to get in and out as fast as possible.

Sighing deeply, she got out of her car and looked up at the sky, it was still pretty bright and sunny. She locked her doors and took the elevators to the second floor. As she approached he opened the door before she could knock.

He smiled at her.

"Marriage suits you well," he smiled like a Cheshire cat.

Jessica entered and stood by the dining room table.

Ignoring his comment, she replied "So I took a look at your account. There are five homes in your investment portfolio. I've requested valuations on all of them so that I can have an idea of the total value. From what I've seen you can take home roughly three mill."

"That's impressive. Thank you."

Jessica removed two papers from her folder. "Here, this is an Engagement Agreement outlining the terms of the sales; I need you to sign these giving me authority to advertise the homes on the market. Also my commission is 6%."

Ron walked around her to his minibar and placed ice in a glass. Her eyes followed him as he walked away.

"Anything to drink?" he asked her.

"No thank you," she was searching her folder for a pen when she felt him behind her. Her blood ran cold.

She turned facing him.

Before she could ask anything, he pounced on her. He tried to kiss her and she turned her face away.

"Ron stop!" She cried. He was persistent.

22

"What are you doing?" she screamed.
He swiftly turned her around, slamming her onto the table and pressed his body into her on the table. "Get off of me," Jessica shouted, she tried pushing up on her arms but his weight stuck her to the table. Ron frantically dropped his pants and spat in his hand and moistened the length of his rock hard erection. He pushed her panties aside and rammed his throbbing wood inside of her, the force knocking her forehead onto the dining room table, Jessica groaned, clenching her teeth together. "Ron, don't!" she begged. Her hands gripped the edge of the table and she could hear its legs scraping on the tile floor as he repeatedly rammed into her, he groped her breasts, expertly pummeling her

creamy centre.

"Ron, please stop," she moaned. His grip on her waist tightened, his fingertips digging holes into her skin. Jessica felt her juices trickling down her thighs as he savagely ripped into her. Within minutes Jessica's sweet centre spasmed and contracted, squeezing Ron's thick wood, her legs buckled under her from sheer ecstasy as she climaxed hard. Ron held her weight up never slowing his rhythm. A satisfied growl escaped his lips as he blasted inside of her.

Ron collapsed on Jessica's back. "I miss fucking you." His breath was catchy and rough. Her blouse was saturated with his perspiration. He slipped out of her, and he reached under her and slid back into her hot slit, he wasn't finished with her just yet, Jessica felt him filling her again, teasing and massaging her walls to another tantalizing orgasm. She lurched backwards, grinding her hips into him, she whimpered as he repeatedly pierced her core taking her over the edge.

She was breathless and panting. Ron assisted her off the table and into the chair, her legs were weak. Her breasts were spilling out of her bra, she adjusted them and buttoned her top. Ron brought her a bottle of water but she was too embarrassed to look at him. She dashed from the dining table with her skirt above her waist and panties askew.

"Where's your bathroom?" she didn't dare make eye contact with him.

He pointed straight ahead. She slammed the bathroom door shut and locked the door.

She cleaned herself off and fixed her clothing. She rested on the door, her hands clasped over her lips, fighting back her screams. She splashed water on her face and tried to tame her hair.

"Fuck." She spent fifteen minutes in the bathroom. She thought of climbing through the bathroom window but it was too small. She unlocked the door, gathered her emotions and returned. Ron was waiting. He was now in different clothing and his face looked freshly washed, he looked relaxed and maybe even a bit smug.

Jessica fixed her folder beneath her arm and walked to the door.

"Jessica wait!" He stretched his hand to stop her.

"Don't touch me," she seethed, she avoided his hand and walked to the door, her wobbly legs barely able to support her.

The key was still in the door; she turned it and unlocked the door. She rushed out of the elevator as fast as she could. Her hands were shaking so badly that she found it difficult to open her car door. She flung the door open and sat in her seat and immediately locked her doors, she scoped out her surroundings and no one was outside. Jessica drove to a nearby Mall and parked. She switched off her ignition. She immediately burst into tears. Her hands were trembling uncontrollably as she wiped away the flood of tears from her eyes. She screamed a high pitched squeal while she shook the steering wheel.

"Fuck Jessica. Whyyyyyy?" she couldn't stop crying. She did not know where to go or who to call.

She needed to shower. She smelled like sex. Horrible thoughts rushed through her mind. He didn't use protection. Shit. He came inside of her twice.

Jessica called Charmaine.

"I need you to get me a Plan B stat," she said shakily.

"What's wrong?" Charmaine asked genuinely concerned.

"I'll explain later. Meet at 7:00 p.m. at the Swanson mall. Bring it then."

"Jessica."

"I'll explain when I see you." Jessica hung up.

She tapped her head against the steering wheel until she felt the beginnings of a terrible headache.

She didn't want to think of the hurt she'd be inflicting on Trey if he ever found out. She needed to reach home before Trey. She started her engine and made a mad dash for home. Thankfully, Max was gone which meant Trey was out taking him for a walk.

She ran up the stairs, undressed and stepped into the shower. She took down her hair and decided to wash it. She lathered her rag and scrubbed her entire body, she stood under the steaming water and gently placed her hand between her legs, she hissed, the hot soapy water stinging her slit. She was sore and bruised. She spent a few more minutes ensuring she removed all traces of Ron.

When she felt clean enough, she turned the water off, stepped out and threw on her robe. She began to blow dry her hair as she sat on the edge of her bed and cried once more. She dried her eyes with her towel and threw her robe off and stood in the mirror, there were red marks on her hips. Got damn. She couldn't let Trey see them. She pulled a long t-shirt and lounge sweats from her drawer.

Jessica would have kicked her own ass if she could.

Trey and Max burst through the door ten minutes later. She gave Trey a peck on the cheek. He filled Max's bowls with water and dog food and sat next to her on the patio.

"How was your day?" he asked.

"It was cool. I'm supposed to meet with Charmaine shortly, so, it'll just be you and Max for a while."

"Ok. I'm gonna hop in the shower before you go. Can you fix me a shake before you run off?"

"Sure!"

"Thanks baby," he kissed her before going up the

stairs.

Jessica blended the shake and placed it in the refridgerator. When he came down from his shower she was ready to go.

"I'm heading out."

"See you later," she pecked him lightly on his lips.

Plucking her keys and jacket from the kitchen counter, she took a bottled water and went out to her car. She sat in her car looking at her home, tears filling her eyes. She shook her head and drove off.

Jessica arrived before her sister, she parked near the entrance so that Charmaine would see her vehicle easily. Seconds later, Charmaine pulled up directly next to sister's car. She exited her car and sat in the passenger seat of Jessica's car.

"What the hell is going on?" Charmaine asked as soon as she closed the door."

Jessica unleashed sudden tears, her body racked with trembling.

"Sissy what's wrong?" Charmaine was afraid.

Jessica was bawling. She was physically shaking.

"Jessica?" Charmaine was now crying. She took her sister in her arms, comforting her reminding that whatever it is, she was there.

Jessica sniffled. "Did you bring it?"

"Yeah!" She dug into her purse and passed her the Plan B box.

Jessica wiped her face with her shirt and popped the box open, she removed it from the packing and swallowed it with a big swig of her water.

"I really fucked up," she said. Pushing air from her mouth she continued. "I fucked up my whole life."

"What happened?" Charmaine's eyes were bugged again.

Jessica looked at her and laughed out loud. It wasnt

the time for laughter but she couldn't help it this time.

She told her sister the complete story of Ron contacting her about the homes she helped him acquire and the fact that he wanted to place them on the market.

"So he invited you over to his Condo this evening? Tell me you didn't sleep with that man girl?" she asked heatedly.

Jessica looked at her sister and nodded.

"Jessica. What the fuck did you do? Oh my Gosh," Charmaine asked angrily. "That's fucked up! How could you do that Trey?"

"I know. I'm so sorry." Jessica stared at the cars entering and exiting the carpark.

"Why the hell did you go over there?"

"I don't know," she paused. "It was supposed to be a business meeting, that's it."

"Oh you know bitch. You got exactly what you went for. Hmmm. What was it? You wanted him to dick you down good one last time. Hmmm. You are dumb as fuck for this."

"I didn't go there to have sex with him," she screamed. Did I? She thought

"Why do you think he asked you over there, huh?" she snapped.

"Char..."

"He wanted to fuck the shit out of you and send you back home to your loving husband. That's why," she barked. Charmaine was pissed off. "And why the hell would you let him come inside you."

"I didn't *let* him come inside me." She felt defeated and she started crying again.

"Are you gonna tell Trey?"

"I can't tell Trey. What am I gonna tell him Charmaine?" Jessica asked frustrated.

"Do you still have feelings for him?"

"No. I don't."

"This isn't good Jess. You've got to tell Trey, you can't let that bitch throw this in his face."

Jessica scoffed. "I can't tell Trey Char. It's over if I do and I don't want to lose him."

"This is too much, even for me."

Jessica sighed heavily.

"You look like shit too. You can't go back home looking like you've been crying" Charmaine was stone faced.

Jessica flipped her sun visor down looking in the small mirror. Her eyes were red and puffy.

"Ohhh. I'm so upset with you. I pray to God you haven't ruined your marriage."

"Believe me, so am I," she wiped her eyes for the millionth time.

"I have get back home. I didn't think I was gonna be this long."

"Thank you."

Charmaine cut her eyes at her sister and stepped out of the car. She should beat the shit out of her for being a dumbass.

23

On her way home, Jessica ran through all of the outcomes of telling Trey. She couldn't come up with one that didn't end in divorce. She got home and Max jumped up on her. She rustled his mane and brushed past him. She eased to the guest bathroom and washed her face. Trey was waiting for her at the door.

"What's wrong?"

"PMS," she lied.

"Oh ok. I made dinner, if you want to eat," he added.

"Sure."

He set two dinner plates on the table and dished out baked pie, fried chicken and green beans.

"Were you crying?" he asked concerned.

"I think it might be an allergic reaction to something

I touched or ate."

"This chicken is bomb," she said, looking down at her plate because she couldn't quite meet his gaze.

"I'm glad you like it," he smiled.

Jessica avoided Trey's glares. He knew she was not being honest with him.

"A few bills and other mail came today."

"I keep forgetting to clear the box. Thanks," she said.

Jessica forced herself to eat. She felt sick and uncomfortable in his presence.

"I'm done," she pushed the plate away.

"You hardly touched your food."

"I'm full hun."

He walked over to her chair and placed her plate in the microwave. She went to the living room and stretched out on the couch. He joined her and began caressing her stomach gently, he moved on top of her and bent to kiss her, she returned his kisses, nibbling on his soft lips. A low moan escaped him. His kisses became more urgent, he slipped his hand inside of her pants and between her legs. Damn, what a fantastic time for him to want to have sex. She couldn't anyway even if she wanted too.

She pushed up off the couch and laid him on his back before straddling him. She trailed kisses along his neck all the way down his stomach to the soft patch above his twitching manhood. She took him in her mouth, his thickness almost choking her. Trey held her hair from her face, observing her, his mouth etched in a permanent 'O' as he savored the hot slippery sensation of her mouth. He delighted in the way her tongue slithered snake-like along his veined shaft. She swirled her tongue along his massive length, teasing him. Trey sighed heavily, becoming even more excited.

"Don't stop!" He growled.

Jessica increased her rhythm, her head bobbing up and down vigorously, her lips pressed firmly against his length and she glided them up and down, she licked his pre cum away as his body stiffened and his toes curled backwards. Jessica heard a loud wail and she flinched when a sweet creamy liquid invaded her throat, she swallowed all of his spilled seed and licked him clean. She continued exploring him with her mouth until he begged her to stop. While he lay catching his breath he signaled for her to lay on his chest. She obliged and rested her head on his chest; she had to give herself props for thinking on her feet.

"That was so damn good baby," he said sheepishly.

"Hmmm" Jessica felt a stab of guilt. She forced herself not to think about what occurred that evening.

"I'll be right back." She rolled over him and went to the bathroom, she took a breath to calm her nerves. She swigged with mouthwash and returned to Trey.

Jessica switched the tv on and settled on a comedy that was tagged with a six star rating, she propped her feet on Trey and they watched tv together until late into the night.

For the next few days she arrived to work earlier than usual, she was avoiding Trey at all costs, at least for the moment. "Hey Syl, who placed this envelope on my desk?" Sylvia was the Receptionist at the front desk.

"It was dropped off by a gentleman before you arrived."

"Ok. Thanks."

Jessica took up the envelope, there was no name or return address noted anywhere. She pulled the tab open and peered inside. There were two sheets of paper inside. She fished them out and began reading. It was the paperwork she took to Ron's four days ago.

Jessica rushed to her boss' office, she knocked on the door and waited for permission to enter.

She stood inside of the door. "Good Morning. I have a big problem."

"What is it?" he removed his glasses and waited for her to continue.

"I can't take this account," she spread the documents out before him.

"Why not? This would be a really great commission," he advised.

"Those belong to Ron...and it's complicated. Please, can you get someone else to handle these?" Jessica's boss was well aware that her relationship with Ron did not end amicably, therefore, he didn't question her further.

"I'll see if Derrick can add these to his accounts."

She shook her head. "Thank you." She opened the door.

"Jessica! Is everything ok?"

"Yes. Thanks." Only if he knew.

It was two months to the day Jessica had slept with Ron. With the help of a therapist she was able to work through her emotions. She had informed Trey that she was feeling very stressed and needed someone professional to speak to. He was aware that she was emotional at times and would often shut down when he pressed her. Jessica's appointments ran for one hour or more depending on her emotional state. She enjoyed the freedom of speaking her mind to an unbiased party.

After one of her appointments she arranged to meet Charmaine for lunch simply to catch up. Their relationship was strained and they weren't spending as much time together like before. Jessica knew that her sister was disappointed in her and was avoiding her as punishment. Charmaine got to the restaurant on time, when she was about to call Jessica to ask where she was, she pulled into the carpark. Charmaine examined her sister from her seat, she knew Jessica was seeing a therapist but she was still a little pissed that she allowed Ron to trick her and use her.

Jessica could feel the tension between her and Charmaine. She missed their playful banter.

"Good Afternoon sister," Jessica said.

"Good Afternoon."

"I've missed you." Jessica said sadly. We hardly see each other."

"I miss you too sissy. I'm not going to deny the way I feel. I'm angry with you and you know why."

"The only thing I can do is apologize and I did."

"How many sessions have you had?" Charmaine wondered.

"Three."

"Is it working for you?

"Yes. I feel much better when I see him."

"That's good," she concluded.

Just then the waitress appeared to take their orders.

"Do you see me differently?" Jessica asked. She was seconds away from crying.

"No. I don't. I guess we all make mistakes." She reached for her sister's hand and squeezed it.

The waitress returned with their drinks. Jessica ordered a Surf's up and Charmaine ordered an Island in the Sun.

"Has he tried calling you?"

"Nope."

"Ok."

The sisters ate and caught up once their food arrived. Charmaine's anniversary was coming up soon and she wanted to borrow an outfit from Jessica's closet.

"Are you sure my clothing can fit you?"

"Of course. We are practically shaped the same way," she chided.

"Bitch! No we're not.

"Yeah, you're right." They both laughed out loud.

"No. But I wanted Jeffrey to see me in something sexy."

"My kinda sexy is too much for him girl."

"I'm still going to come over and check," she said.

"Fine, you can come when we leave," Jessica said.

They ended their meal and Jessica slipped to the bathroom while Charmaine paid the bill.

They exited the restaurant.

"See you home in 20 minutes," Charmaine said.

"Yeah, cool."

They left the carpark en route to Jessica's. When Jessica pulled up to her curb, Trey's car was parked outside. Strange she thought. He probably ended work early.

Jessica waited in her car until Charmaine drove up. When she saw her sister's blue Rav4 she stepped out and waited by her trunk. Charmaine parked behind Jessica and exited. Stepping through the door she could hear Trey's anguished voice flowing down the hall.

Jessica entered the kitchen as Trey ended his call.

"Why were you at Ron's place a few months ago?" he shouted.

"What?" His question startled her.

"Jessica, why were you at Ron's house two months ago," he said slowly and deliberately.

"I should go." Charmaine turned to leave.

"Don't go Charmaine. I bet you know why your sister was at her ex's house." He glared at Jessica. He was seething.

"Wait. I can explain," her throat was dry and hot.

Tears stinging her eyes.

"Go ahead," he bellowed.

"He wanted to sell his properties that I initially helped him purchase when we were together and he said that he wanted to sell them so I..I.. took the paper work over to his house." She rushed the words out just to get them out.

"So you couldn't have had him come to the office?" he barked.

Jessica sat at the kitchen Island facing him.

"He asked me to visit him at his home. It's not an uncommon request," she offered.

"Did you fuck him?" he asked, his eyes glistening.

Jessica felt sick. She didn't know whether to lie or tell him truth.

"Just tell me the truth. Did you have sex with him or not?" he asked. His blood was boiling.

24

"Trey..."

"Just answer the fucking question," he screamed at her.

"Yes," she said softly, she felt physically ill.

Their eyes locked on each other, hate and confusion written all over Trey's face.

"Trey, I'm so sorry." Jessica was crying profusely.

"Sorry. You're sorry." He was disgusted just looking at her.

She walked over to where he was standing.

"Did you use protection?"

Jessica ran her hands through her hair. She didn't answer.

"It didn't happen the way you think," she said trying to persuade him.

"Did he make you cum? Cause if you did, that means you enjoyed it, right!"

"That's not how it happened," she said crying harder.

"I can't believe you would do this to me."

"I'm sorry baby. I didn't mean for this to happen," she cried.

"You wanted it, just say it."

"I didn't want to sleep with him," she pleaded.

"Then why the fuck would you go over to his home?" he screamed again.

"It wasn't to sleep with him, I promise you."

"You've always loved that man. I saw you at the airport, you two couldn't keep your eyes off of each other. You thought I didn't notice?" he shouted, appalled that she would lie and cheat on him.

"I love you and only you. I swear I don't love him," she wiped her tears away with her hands.

"You fucked him two weeks after we got married. Two fucking weeks," he bellowed.

"I'm sorry."

"Why didn't you tell me?"

"How was I gonna tell you I had sex with Ron, I couldn't."

"I'm done," he said as he headed to the stairs.

"Trey, please don't go, not like this," she said panicked.

Jessica tried to stop him from leaving but he pushed her out of his way.

"Trey! Trey." She bawled after him.

Jessica raced up the stairs chasing him. He dragged his suitcase from the closet and started flinging clothing into it.

"Please don't go," she begged

He was no longer listening to her.

He threw the suitcase down the stairs and ran down

behind it.

He snatched his keys from the counter, tousled Max's hair and slammed the door shut as he walked out.

Jessica sat at the bottom of the stairs, the tears now drenching her top. She drew her knees to her chest, the harsh cries racking her body. Max came whimpering to Jessica, he was hungry. She sniffled and wiped her nose in her shirt sleeve and eventually got up and filled both of his bowls with food and water. She tried calling Trey's cell but it was turned off. She took a glass and filled it halfway with rum. She sat on the patio sipping it slowly, the strong heat from the alcohol burning the back of her throat making her cough incessantly. She called Trey again, still no answer.

By 11:00 p.m., she still couldn't reach Trey, she was worried. By 2:00 a.m., his phone was turned on but he refused to take her calls. At 6:00 a.m., he sent her to voicemail.

Jessica had not spoken to Trey in two days, she felt distraught. She was unable to focus at work and not hearing him was stressing her out, she felt alone and scared. She made an appointment to see her therapist as soon as possible. Jessica was becoming desperate. One week later and she was still unable to find her husband. She was certain that his best friend Cameron would know where he was, so she grabbed the telephone directory and searched his name. She found it within seconds. She dialed his number, hoping he would take her call. Her prayers were answered.

"Hi Cameron. This is Jessica. Uhmm, how are you? Uhhh I'm trying to find Trey, have you heard from him? We had a huge argument and I haven't heard him all week," she asked anxiously.

"He's fine. He's staying at a hotel," he said.

"Where?"

Jessica heard him exhaling, pushing air from his mouth. "I can't tell you, he asked me not to tell you if you called. I'm sorry Jessica."

"How is he?" she asked scared to hear his reply.

"He's hurting. Look I'll tell him that you called. Just give him some time."

"Thanks Cam," she ended the call. She knew she'd hurt him bitterly. He probably never wanted to see her again.

Hours later, Trey called her.

"Cam is going to pick up Max later," he said.

"Can we talk?"

"No. Jessica," he ended the call.

Jessica felt emotionally drained, she left work early so that she could cry in peace. She flew under her bed covers and cried until she had no more tears left to cry.

Cameron collected Max around 7:00 p.m. that night. She was tempted to follow him to the hotel to see where Trey was staying but she changed her mind, she didn't want to risk him seeing her, infuriating him even more than he already was.

Jessica missed Max, at least he offered her a little company when Trey was not there. She was alone. How would she explain this to her family. It was all too much to bear.

Loud anguished sobs rattled her core. Why did she go over there? Did she subconsciously want to have sex with Ron? No. She didn't. She took her phone out and dialed Trey's number one more time. No answer. Jessica's wails lessened. She walked into her bedroom and lay on top of her covers for a few seconds. She soon undressed and took a quick shower and spent the rest of the evening trying to reach her husband.

She had dozed off and the ringing of her phone woke her from her nap.

"Hey. You still haven't heard him yet?" Charmaine asked.

"He's staying in a hotel, his friend Cameron told me."

"At least he's ok, you know."

"Yea."

"You need to tell him what really happened," she said cautiously.

"Char, don't. I told you he didn't rape me," she said angrily.

"If you told him no, that's rape Jessica."

"I came twice Char, if he had raped me I wouldn't have climaxed," she was baffled by Charmaine's comments.

"So what, you told him 'no' and you told him so more than once," Charmaine said annoyed.

On any other day Jessica would have cussed her sister the hell out.

"I don't want to talk about this anymore, I'll call you tomorrow." "Bitch!" Jessica said under her breath.

Jessica was of the opinion that even though she said no to Ron's advances, she did climax once or twice, she could not remember. She did not really enjoy the sex, or did she, it was painful, so why did she climax. She was very confused.

Charmaine came over unexpectedly at 3:00 p.m. the next day. Jessica opened the door and returned to her bed, ignoring her sister.

"Why are you still in bed on a Saturday afternoon?"

"What do you want?"

"I came to see you, why else?"

"You could have called," she said full of attitude.

"Have you eaten, I brought lunch." Charmaine offered ignoring her stink attitude.

"I'm not hungry." Jessica was staring at the

television.

Charmaine rushed at her sister, dragging her from the bed all the way to the top of the stairs.

"Get your ass downstairs," she barked.

"Charmaine let me go!" she screamed.

"No," she shouted back.

Before Charmaine could drag her down the stairs, Jessica kicked her legs out, hitting Charmaine on her shoulder.

"Ouch bitch." Charmaine was breathing hard. She sat on the top stairs next to her sister, who was stretched out, not moving.

"Jess, I think you have to tell Trey that Ron raped you."

Jessica rolled her eyes and sat up on her elbows to face her sister.

"After Ron was finished, I came too. How do I explain that to him?" Water settled in her eyes."

"You have to try, sissy."

"He wouldn't talk to me anyway," she cried.

"Let's go eat." Charmaine helped her sister up and went into the hallway and brought the Styrofoam containers into the living room.

They unpacked the lunches on the coffee table.

"Call him now, see if he answers."

"No."

"Please."

Sighing, she said, "I gotta get my phone." Jessica dashed upstairs, hastily grabbed her phone and sat next to her sister. She punched Trey's number and placed the call on speaker so that Charmaine could hear. The call was directed to voicemail.

"See?" Jessica said.

"Hmm. Can you get me some ketchup and some ice?"

Once Jessica was gone, Charmaine cautiously

picked up Jessica's cell and opened her call log, she quickly wrote down Trey's cell number in her notepad and stealthily replaced the phone where it was.

"Here," she rested the glass with ice and ketchup on the coffee table.

Jessica flicked the remote on, searching for a show to watch.

"Olivia has a bon fire something or the other coming up." Jessica stated.

"You going?" Charmaine asked.

"I really don't want too, I'm not in the mood to answer a gazillion questions and I feel kinda embarrassed," she stated.

"That's your family, we will always have your back no matter what."

Jessica smiled.

"I'm gonna wait and see how I feel," she said focusing on scooping up her chicken fried rice.

Charmaine nodded, her mouth too full to respond.

"You're a nasty eater, ewwww," Jessica said, her face set in a scornful manner.

Charmaine gave her sister the middle finger.

25

Charmaine started her engine, she was parked outside of her sister's home. She slid the notepad from her purse staring at Trey's number. She took a glance at Jessica's home and back at the number. She hurriedly punched his number, he answered on the third ring.

"Trey, this is Charmaine. There's something I believe you need to know."

The call lasted twenty minutes. Before hanging up, she pleaded with him not to tell her sister that she had told him. Charmaine pulled satisfied she did what she thought was best.

Jessica knew that when life got hard, she had to work harder. She was working overtime almost every day. There was nothing or no one to run home to.

She was on top of her game. No room for error.

Her commissions doubled and she grossed the highest gross earnings for the Quarter. Sadly, her marriage had ended before it had even started. She hated when people asked her how Trey was doing. She always gave them a general answer because she didn't even know herself. She stopped calling him, as her therapist suggested.

She took a short break from working and stood by her office window watching the traffic whizz by. She popped into the staff kitchen and poured herself a cup of tea and sat at the lunch table sipping her hot brew. Jessica knew they were rumours around the office of her possible impending divorce and her having an affair with a mystery man, the said reason for her divorce.

She stood, taking her coffee with her back to her office walking by her boss' open door.

"Ah, Jessica, a second please," he called.

She stepped in and propped against the door. He signaled for her to sit. She closed the door behind her and took a seat across from him.

"Are the rumors true?" Jessica felt the hairs on her neck stand up.

She rolled her neck "I didn't have an affair and Trey and I are..," she paused, searching for the right word..."we are,..it's complicated."

"Do you need time off?" he asked.

"I'd go insane being at home with nothing to do," she sighed.

"If there's anything I can do, let me know." His offer was genuine.

"Thanks boss!" she said smiling.

In her office, she pulled up her open reports and began editing. She opened her calendar next, sifting through her upcoming appointments for the month;

her mouse idled over her sister's bon fire event. It was set for 8:00 p.m. three weeks from Friday. By the time the event arrived, she decided to go, after all it was her family. She left work early, she wanted to rest a little before she left for her sister's home, she was burnt out and frazzled. She dropped her purse and work bag in the hall and rested on her living room floor. Within minutes she was fast asleep. She slept for four hours straight. When she woke, it was dark out.

Jessica stretched lazily, she felt renewed and energized, her elation was short lived when she recalled that her actions ultimately ruined her marriage. She had not heard from Trey in weeks. She knew it was over, sadly at her own hands. She climbed the stairs to her bedroom and undressed. She would shower later when she got ready for the bon fire. She flitted around in her bra and panties, folding clean laundry and vacuuming her bedroom. She then entered her closet searching for a warm outfit. She selected a pair of black jeans and a maroon hoodie sweatshirt pairing them with black sneakers.

Placing her outfit on the bed, she removed her panties, tossing them in the laundry basket. She stepped into the shower and adjusted the temperature to cool. When was finished, she turned the water off and toweled her skin dry. She dressed and sat at her vanity, she decided to wear her hair loose and curly and no makeup. She was tired of being home alone and wanted to be in the company of others, so at 7:00 p.m. she was on her way to Olivia's home.

"Hello ladies." Jessica greeted her sisters. They were seated in lounge chairs around the fire pit in a semi-circle.

"Hey Jess," They all said. They individually hugged her. They'd decided before she came not to question her about her marriage, from the little snippets

Charmaine fed them, her marriage was in shambles. A banquet table was set up under the covered patio and Jessica filled a plate with chips, biscuits and a slice of cake and sat in the chair next to Alexus.

"As I was saying, I'm thinking of getting my nipples pierced," Olivia stated happily.

"Both?" Rebecca asked.

"No girl, one for now. I'm doing it on Thursday next week," she added.

"Who are you going to?" Alexus asked.

"My tattoo artist, duh," Olivia said.

Jessica was enjoying the camaraderie of her sisters.

They spent the next two hours bonding and catching up. The air was ice cold, the heat from the fire barely reducing the cold night air. As they chatted, a familiar male voice said "Good night."

They all swiveled their heads, startled by the voice. It was Trey. Everyone was stunned except Charmaine. Each sister turned to look at Jessica who was flabbergasted.

"Let's give them some privacy," Charmaine said.

"Good night Trey." They each said as they walked past him.

Alexus, Rebecca, Charmaine and Olivia gathered their plates and went into the house, but kept a visual on their sister, just in case. Sisters for life!

Trey sat next to Jessica. He looked so handsome. She wanted to hug him, she wanted to kiss him but she knew he'd push her away and she couldn't stand if he rejected her.

"Goodnight," he said to her.

"Goodnight," she said. They gazed at each other for a long moment. Jessica looked away.

"Cam told me you called again," he said. He kept his eyes locked on her, each moment unbearable for her.

"You wouldn't talk to me so I called him."

"I wasn't ready to talk." He shifted to lean on his knees.

"Where do we stand?" she asked. Her breath caught in her throat.

"I don't know Jessica."

Jessica was sitting lotus style with her plate nestled in her lap.

"Do you want a divorce?" Jessica propped her head back allowing her tears to roll into her loose hair. She swiftly wiped her eyes hoping he didn't notice.

"I don't know that either," he said softly.

Jessica knew that her betrayal cut him like a knife, she hoped it didn't cost her everything.

"I'm sorry that I hurt you and embarrassed you," she desperately needed to hold him, take his unhappiness away. She inhaled before continuing, "I didn't go over there to have sex with him. I hope you know that."

"I feel like I don't know anything anymore."

"Why are you here?" she asked softly.

"We need to talk."

"How did you know I was here?"

"Charmaine told me." Jessica glanced at the kitchen window, she saw Charmaine quickly step away from sight.

Trey rested his head on his clasped hands. An uncomfortable silence shrouded them.

"You really broke me."

"I know and it's the one thing I'll always regret." She ached to comfort him, to reassure him.

Agonizing cries, painful and heartbreaking escaped from him.

Jessica rushed over to him. She knelt on her knees before him dabbing his tears away with her napkin.

"I'm so sorry Trey. I never meant to hurt you," she wrapped her arms around him, her face snug against his, his tears now mingling with hers. He eased his head on her shoulder, shuddering as his heart broke.

She whispered in his ears. "I love you so much." Trey angled his head up searching for her lips, their lips touched, he kissed her hungrily. He cupped her face in his hands, the desire for her overpowering him. He moaned as she bit the soft flesh of his lips. His hands caressed her breasts through her sweatshirt and her hands tightened around him, his lips pressing harder against hers. "I need you now," he said breathlessly. He released her face and dropped his hands to her jeans.

He began to unzip her jeans.

"Trey!" Jessica held his hands.

He looked at her in a daze.

"Not here."

"Where then?" he asked.

"Home!"

He looked away. "Jess, I don't want to give you any ideas. I'm not ready for..."

She kissed him softly on his lips. "I know. We'll take it slow," she said softly.

Jessica stood and dusted the grass off her jeans, she noticed her sisters scampering from the window. She smiled.

"I'm gonna tell them I'm leaving." She picked up her plate and tossed the remains in the kitchen garbage can.

"Guy's I'm leaving!" she said bashfully.

Trey entered behind her. His eyes were red. They recognized Jessica and Trey had both been crying. He saluted to them and exited the kitchen and waited for Jessica at her car. Since they drove separately, they would meet at home. They pulled up to her curb, Trey parking behind her. She locked her car and Trey followed suit. She unlocked her front door and they both stepped inside.

Jessica offered him something to drink or eat. Neither was hungry, so they sat on the couch, silent.

"Where are you staying?" she asked.

"The Sentinnel Hotel on Coward Road."

"Do you love me?" he suddenly blurted.

"What kind of question is that?"

"Just answer." He was intense.

She faced him. "Yes. I love you. I love you more than you know," she said assuredly. He was silent again, thinking.

"Jess, I want to ask you something, but I need you to answer me honestly." He said sternly.

Jessica felt overwhelmed and anxious, her armpits were dripping with perspiration under her shirt.

"What?"

"Did he rape you?" he asked.

Jessica made a silent promise to kick Charmaine's ass.

26

Jessica stared at Trey, running her answers through her mind. Every time she opened her mouth to respond she closed her mouth shut.

"Just say it," he said.

"I don't know 100%." She hung her head in shame. She didn't want to see the loathing he felt for her plastered on his face.

"What happened when you went over there?"

"I can't tell you," she said shaking her head. Her soul felt crushed and she began to cry.

"I'm not here to judge you, I just need to know, please."

Jessica wiped her eyes and straightened her back before she began. She replayed the entire sordid scenario to Trey, including the parts that crippled her to repeat. He listened intently as she spoke, his face contorting and tensing as she told her story.

"You should have told me you were going there."

"I never thought that he would hurt me, far less in that way," she wiped her nose, sniffling.

"Hmm, where on 4th Avenue does he live?" he asked as nonchalantly as possible.

"Why?" Jessica's eyes flew up to his face as soon as he asked her that question. Alarm bells going off in her ears.

"It doesn't matter," she said.

"Jessica, where on 4th Avenue does Ron live?" he asked even more demanding.

"Trey, I don't think that it's a good idea for you to know,"

"Cool." Jessica knew what that 'cool' meant, he was annoyed. "I'm sorry that happened to you Jess."

She nodded her head slightly.

"I've got to go." He stood and waited for her.

She stood, took his face in her hands and pressed her lips firmly against his, they shared a long lingering kiss, his hands palming her curvy body. She felt his manhood hard against her stomach.

He broke their embrace, "Jessica."

"Ok," sighing, she backed off. She desperately craved her husband but she didn't want to push him. She walked him to the door and watched him leave. A single tear slipped from her eye before she had closed the door.

Three months later, Trey was still living in an apartment. He would seldom visit Jessica at home or they would have the occasional lunch date or chat on the phone. He was not ready for anything more serious and Jessica understood. They discussed counseling but Trey was apprehensive about the idea.

"Turn on your television now." Charmaine said excitedly.

Jessica ran to her living room and switched the television on. The nightly news was showing. The news reporter was reading a briefing on prominent businessman Ron Bishop's horrific assault and robbery attempt outside of his 4th Avenue home. He was currently in hospital in critical condition.

"Oh my God!" Jessica gasped.

"Girl, did you see that shit. Karma is a bitch." Charmaine was hyped.

"When did this happen?"

"A few days ago it seems," she replied.

Jessica thought of Trey instantly.

"Char, lemme call you later."

Jessica sunk into her couch, she immediately tried reaching Trey on his cell. No answer. Her heart was racing. She prayed Trey was not involved in Ron's assault. She tried googling the news story on the internet but no new information was available as yet.

Trey called her shortly after she had called him.

"Where are you?"

"Home, the hotel," he said.

"Did you watch the news?"

"Yes. Enjoyed it thoroughly," he said haughtily.

"Trey!" She was alarmed.

"Why do you care so damn much?" he was irritated.

"I don't. I don't want you involved in any bullshit," she said guardedly.

"Everything is fine Jess."

"Is it really? Jessica wanted to wring his neck in that

moment, his attitude pissed her off completely, she was getting nowhere with him.

"It is."

She hung up on him without another word and called her sister. "Any other news?"

"Yes. He was rushed to theatre for emergency surgery, his lungs collapsed."

Shit! She thought.

"Any suspects?" she asked biting her nails.

"Nope."

"Anyway, are you getting anywhere with Trey?"

"Slowly. I guess." Jessica was too worried about Trey's involvement with Ron's assault to focus on their marital woes.

She spent the rest of the week ceremoniously checking the news reports on Ron's condition and the suspect's identity or identities.

Late Sunday evening, she felt so overwhelmed that she filled her tub with piping hot water, adding special oils and salts, to take a soak. Jessica stepped into the tub and smiled. The extremely hot water felt so good to her that she stuck her entire body beneath the soothing sudsy water. She resurfaced and settled back against the porcelain tub and closed her eyes. She then took her loofah and washed her body.

Just then, there was a knock on her door.

"Shitttt." She splashed around in anger spilling water to the floor. There was another knock, this time louder. Jessica got out of the tub, flinging soapy suds from her body with her hands. She tied her robe around her and squeezed the excess water from her hair. She marched downstairs and peered through the peephole, before opening the door.

"Hi," she said, stunned.

"Hi," he said, swaying on his heels.

"Come in. I was upstairs," she stepped back

allowing him in.

Trey stepped in and locked the door after him.

"I can see that," he said taking in her wet silhouette.

"Let me wash off. I'll be right back."

"Ok."

Jessica ran upstairs and hopped in the shower. When she returned, Trey was in her room. He closed the door and leaned against it taking her in.

"You're so beautiful," he said as she towel dried her hair. She sat at her vanity brushing out the tangles.

"Jessica, come here."

She paused slightly, then pushed her chair back and turned to focus on him.

Trey had walked up closely behind her. He sat her on her vanity. He rubbed his nose against her cheeks before sliding his lips to hers, he kissed her lips roughly, eagerly, his breath catching in hers. Jessica's body flinched as he slipped two fingers between her legs, rubbing her slit alive.

She loosened his shorts hurriedly; it fell to the floor with a thud. He eased her upright and rested her ass on the top of her vanity. Their kisses intensified as he darted his fingers in and out of her wetness, he pulled his fingers out and tasted her juices, the more he licked and sucked on his shiny fingertips, the more her slit creamed and spasmed. He then slipped his fingers into her mouth letting her taste her own essence. Trey lowered his head and playfully sucked on her breasts as he spread her legs wider. Swiftly he gripped her legs and lifted them over his arms and penetrated her deeply, attacking her delicious centre. His lips found hers again and he repeatedly slammed his rock hard length inside of her. After more than two months with no physical contact from him, she felt like she was going insane. Filthy noises grumbled from her lips as he massaged her walls with quickness and delightful speed.

Trey held her legs tightly, his strokes tearing into softness, sending her into a frenzy. Jessica rolled her hips faster, wildly rising and falling against his hardness, her walls tightened and contracted and she shrieked, the pleasure of her climax radiating throughout her body. Her erotic whimpers sent Trey ballistic and he came instantly, his cum spilling out of him, he gasped and heaved until he was finally able to remove his pulsating manhood from her.

"Fuckkkkk", he said, as he took a few steps away from her, droplets of cum, seeping onto her extended thigh. He stretched for a wipe from her vanity and squeezed the excess cum into the wipe and cleaned himself off.

Jessica teetered off her vanity, she flung her towel over her shoulder and returned to her shower. She hastily rinsed off and dried her body. Wrapping the towel round her, she stepped into the bedroom. She dressed in a pair of shorts and tank top. When she returned Trey was dressed and sitting on the bed. He did not look up as she entered the room.

"Do you want something to drink?"

"Yea, I have a bottle of red in the refridgerator. I'll be down shortly."

He headed to the kitchen and placed the glasses and the bottle of wine on the coffee table. Jessica came in and sat on the floor next to him. He had the fireplace going and the lights were down low.

"I want you to come back home," she said softly, observing his reaction to what she said.

"That's been heavy on my mind," he confessed.

"So, what's stopping you?"

Trey chugged his glass of wine.

He scooted down on the floor next to her. He held

her hand on his legs. "Nothing is stopping me, I miss you. I miss us and Max misses you too. He's been giving me hell."

They shared a mild chuckle together.

"I miss him too." She massaged his beard with her free hand and pressed her elbows on his legs. Her lips kissed him softly, then urgently, her insides quivered in anticipation of more. His hand caressed the back of her neck, pulling her in closer.

She pulled away, "I love kissing you," she said.

He pulled her back to him again, kissing her eagerly. He missed her terribly, it felt as though he was making up for lost time. He laid on his back and she straddled him, they kissed intensely while his hands found their way under her shorts. He squeezed her butt, slapping her soft flesh ever so often. Her excitement grew as she felt the sudden burgeoning bulge in his pants. Her kisses became now feverish and wild, she pressed her hips into him dry-humping him. She stood up and kicked her shorts off. Kneeling again, she pulled his engorged shaft from his pants, and guided him inside of her. She braced her hands on his chest, and rode him exquisitely, her butt smacked against his jeans as she bounced her tight slit aggressively down on him. Jessica screamed as her body convulsed "Oh my God, I'm coming," her hips thrashed and flailed hypnotically as she came fast and strong, she collapsed on top of him for a few seconds, slowly she rolled off of him straight onto her back. Trey kneeled over her and plunged full force into her depth, filling her entirely, his passionate cries echoing as soon he exploded inside of her.

He flopped between her legs, breathless. Jessica pulled the throw from the couch and covered their nakedness. They remained on the living room floor catching their breaths. Shortly after, they soon fell asleep still naked beneath the throw.

27

They awoke on the floor, cuddled together, spooning. Trey held Jessica closely, snuggling his nose in her loose hair.

"I think we should give our marriage another chance," he said.

"I'm happy to hear that, we can get over this...hurdle."

"I'll go back to the hotel and get my stuff and come back."

"While you do that, I have some errands to run."

"Breakfast?"

"Only eggs for me, thanks."

He patted her thighs and got up. Jessica could hear pots and pans clanging together in the kitchen, she flipped the fireplace off and rolled over on her back.

The smell of eggs cooking made her stomach roar. She searched for the tv remote, she spotted it lodged beneath the couch, she switched the tv on but thought better to freshen up first.

She threw her panties in the wash and went to her bathroom and cleaned up quickly. She returned and sat on the floor again, flipping through the channels. Trey brought her breakfast and a big cup of coffee. He returned with his breakfast of sausage, eggs and toast. They sat on the floor next to each other planning out the next few days. Trey would move back in and they would gradually rebuild their life together.

"I don't want you to ever see him again," he said, his eyes squinted as he said it.

"I don't want to ever see him again, rest assured," she said, taking some of her egg up on a fork.

"Good. I don't trust him".

"He's not gonna be doing anything to anyone for a while," she took in his demeanor. Trey didn't budge.

"What time are you leaving?" he asked.

"As soon as I'm done here."

They finished breakfast and tossed the dirty dishes in the sink. Trey went to shower and Jessica changed her top to something more flashy but kept her shorts on. Trey came into the room just as she was leaving. He noticed her outfit but kept silent. Jessica was wearing a white midriff top and grey cut off shorts, which left little to the imagination.

"See you later," she pecked him on his lips and picked her jacket from the couch.

"Be safe," he said.

Jessica got in her car and dialed Charmaine as she pulled off. She gleefully announced to her that Trey was moving back in. Charmaine was super excited and told Jessica not to fuck it up again. Jessica swung into her usual beauty supply store parking lot, she needed to restock on a few essentials. She was browsing the isles when she heard an unfamiliar voice say her name. She looked to her left, smiling, the smile quickly vanished from her face.

"Hello Jessica," the voice said.

"Hello Lydia," she said warily.

Lydia glowered at Jessica for a few seconds.

"Is there a problem?" Jessica asked amused.

"You do know you're not the first young thing he's had an itching for," Lydia said smugly.

"What do you want Lydia?" she sighed.

"No matter how much pussy you try to trick him with, he's never going to leave me."

"*Trick* him, bitch you must be crazy." Jessica chuckled sinisterly.

"He told me about your little rendezvous at his home."

"Let me stop you right there. I don't give two fucks what he told you," Jessica said snidely.

"Keep away from my husband," Lydia said triumphantly.

"Bitch, fuck you and your hoe ass husband," Jessica said and walked away to finish her shopping. Jessica was boiling inside, she halted and turned to Lydia "And another thing, if you ever approach me again on some Ron shit I'm gonna beat your mother fucking ass." Jessica stalked off to the register and cashed out. Too upset to do anything else, she headed home.

Jessica sped out of the carpark, she was heated. By the time she reached home, steam was flying out her ears.

"How dare she accuse me of seducing Ron," she screamed.

"Babes, I'm back." Trey yelled from the front door.

"I'm in the kitchen!" she shouted.

Max bounded into the kitchen at the sound of her voice. "Maxxxx," she cried, "I missed you," she said running her hand over his shiny coat. Max barked and tried jumping on her leg. "No, Max. Down," he sprinted back to Trey barking once more.

"It's a little early in the day isn't it?" Jessica was pouring herself a shot of Hennessy.

Actually, this was her third shot of the strong Cognac. She pointed a finger at him and downed another one.

"Hey, what's wrong?" he asked concerned. He stepped to her and recorked the bottle. "What happened?"

"Ron's ex approached me just now in the beauty supply store, literally accusing me of seducing his bitch ass." Jessica was practically hollering at Trey.

"Ok calm down."

He led her onto the couch.

"I am calm," she shouted. "I'm sorry, I didn't mean to shout at you."

"I get that she upset you baby, but she's not worth your aggravation. Come on, let's go out for lunch."

"I'm not in the mood, can we order in."

"Sure, what do you feel like eating?"

"Chinese?"

"Sounds good to me!" he said.

Trey tossed her the directory to place the order which took her less than ten minutes. She relaxed on the couch, the Hennessey taking over her body. Their order arrived and she dug in. After her stomach was full, she took a nap on the floor. Trey ate silently while she slept, he grabbed his laptop and opened an electrical drawing which he recently received for a new project.

28

With Trey back home, Jessica slowed down tremendously at work. They spent even more time together than before and she also got around to setting a date for them to go on their honeymoon.

Life was slowly returning to normal. She read in one of the daily newspapers that Ron's surgery was successful, he was in stable condition and might be released from the hospital soon, but he would need some form of physical therapy to fully recover from his injuries. Jessica felt no compassion for Ron. She folded the newspaper and prepared for her 3:00 p.m. showing. She went to the washroom and freshened up her makeup and reapplied her lipstick. She immediately felt lightheaded. "Woah," she said. Her father always warned her about over working and stressing herself out. She returned to her desk and took two sinus tablets just in case her sinuses wanted to act up.

After her showing, she called her boss and told him she was ill and going straight home. She undressed in her bedroom and rested on her bed, soon falling asleep. When Trey came in from work, he found her lying in the bed.

"Hey baby." Trey said kissing her on her cheek.

"What time is it?"

"6:00 o'clock. How long have you been home?"

"Long. I wasn't feeling well so I ended early."

"What's wrong?" he asked as he undressed.

"I'm not sure, I felt really dizzy today, that is why I came home early."

"Well maybe you need to slow down some," he looked at her quizzically.

"I have slowed down," she said flustered.

"Maybe you should see your doctor."

"I might have too."

Jessica made an appointment with her doctor and tried pushing through the rest of the week without taking any days off. She felt tired and achy all week long and she crashed as soon as she got home that Friday evening. Taking two Tylenol, she slept the rest of the evening. When she awoke, she was feeling a tad bit better.

"There's some leftover soup in the refridgerator, I can warm that up for you?"

"Ok. Not too hot though."

Trey pulled a shirt loose from his drawer and went to the kitchen. He placed the cold soup into the microwave for four minutes and took it up to her on a tray, sitting it next to her on the bed.

"I've got to pack this shit up," he was referring to his

belongings from the hotel. Jessica had no plans on assisting him, she recalled begging him to stay when he found out about her and Ron and all of her calls to him going unanswered.

While Trey repacked his clothing, she texted Charmaine, she was busy cooking dinner so they only spoke for a few minutes. She was bored, so she opted for some tv and found a comedy series from the 80's, she sipped on her soup, cackling with laughter. Trey finished packing away his clothing and cuddled next to Jessica, he sampled her soup and handed it back to her.

"I heard your boy got out of the hospital," he said in a sarcastic tone.

"He's not my boy Trey," she said harshly.

"Yea, you're right. I'm sorry," he felt remorseful.

"I don't like that shit, don't do it again."

He held his hands up in surrender. "I'm sorry, that was uncalled for," he stated profusely.

Jessica was upset again. She needed to blow off some steam. She placed her half eaten bowl of soup on the table and changed out of her clothes and pulled on her sports bra and shorts. She took her yoga mat and spread it open in the patio. She stretched and did a ten minute warm up. She laid flat on the mat and did a killer abdominal routine, she then flipped over on her knees and did a booty blast challenge she found on the internet. She ended her workout with an intense cardio burn and forty minutes later, she was drenched in sweat. She did her final stretches and rested flat on the mat.

Jessica rolled her mat up and set it in the corner, she then went to her bathroom and filled her tub, tossing in her herbs and salts, she deserved a nice soak. She ignored Trey who was sitting watching the tv.

She placed her cell on the tiled floor of the bathroom and undressed. She stepped into the piping hot water, she loved the soothing heat. Jessica was offended by Trey's words, hurt actually. She fought the urge to cry, instead she picked her phone up and opened her music library to listen to her favourite tracks.

When the water turned cold, she emerged and toweled off. She took her robe and slung it on. She sat at her vanity and piled her hair atop her head; she applied her facial oils to her face and neck and body oils to her supple skin.

She was amazed at how much better she felt. Trey came up while she was searching her drawers for a particular silky pajama shorts set. She plucked the black strappy set from its hiding place the shimmied into it. She knew Trey was eyeing her so she seductively bent over and stepped into her shorts. She purposely wore no panties as she slid them up her ample curves. She turned, pretending to look for something, displaying her perky breasts, she raised her top above her head letting it fall gracefully over her chest.

She slipped under the covers and continued her tv show. She asked him to turn the lights off downstairs. He came back and laid next to her on his pillow. He knew she was pissed and he was ashamed about his comment, he wanted to avoid further conflict so he said nothing more.

Trey couldn't sleep, it was 1:00 a.m. and he was tossing and turning. He was horny and his wife was upset with him. He ran his hand along her curves and kissed her neck. The subtle gesture was not enough to wake her. He groped her breasts under her nightie set. She shifted slightly.

"Jessica!" He moaned.

"Mmmm," she raised her head, listening to him. "Are you asleep?"

Jessica felt his hand kneading her breasts. She faced him in the semi-darkness. He kissed her gently at first, his finger hooking into the top of pajama bottoms dragging them down her thighs. His moans became needy, he broke from her and knelt above her, she felt his tongue inside of her, swirling, in and out, sending her manic. Jessica squirmed against his tongue as he lashed her velvety softness, her climax came in seconds, she closed her thighs tightly against his head and rode his face, she cried out as waves of incredible pleasure pulsated through her core. She released his head and he slowly trailed kisses from between her legs, over her breasts and to her lips, she tasted her own juices on his tongue. He mounted her, driving his enlarged erection into her silky slit, he pounded her skillfully. She dug her nails into him leaving long scratches on his lower back. His kisses were feverish and he moaned into her mouth as he felt the surge of his climax, he flooded her insides with his creamy nut. "Damn," he said, he fell next to her breathing hard, his stomach trembling with each breath.

Jessica turned on her side, draping his arm over her. He spooned with her, quickly falling asleep until daybreak.

In the coming days, Jessica was still feeling ill, thankfully she was on her way to her appointment. She pressed the doorbell to her Doctor's office and at the sound of the click she entered and spoke to the Receptionist. She was asked to sign in and wait to be called. Ten minutes later, she was seated before Doctor

Crichlow. They went through the usual monotonous routine; she explained her symptoms and the Doctor checked her blood pressure and blood sugar levels before giving her a full examination.

"Are you pregnant?" Dr. Crichlow asked.

Jessica was taken aback.

"I don't think so," she said

"When was your last cycle?

"The 12th February," she answered from memory.

"Are your cycles regular?" the Doctor continued.

"For the most part, yes," she offered.

"Ok. So what we'll do is take a blood sample, run some tests and get back to you as soon as possible. I'll have the nurse come in and take your blood sample."

"Ok." Jessica was nervous, she never considered the possibility.

"Ok then. I'll talk to you later."

Doctor Crichlow stood and exited, the Nurse came in a few seconds later. She took Jessica's blood and informed her that she could return to reception. Jessica thanked her and made her way to reception where she paid for her visit and returned home. She updated Trey when he came home that evening. Her rubbed her back and chest with Vicks Vapour Rub and laid with her until she fell asleep.

Three days later, Jessica sat at her desk browsing through paperwork she needed to close on a sale.

Her cell rang. It was Doctor Crichlow.

"Good Evening Mrs. Sommers, it's Doctor Crichlow," she said, "I have the results of your blood work."

"Ok." Jessica was holding her breath.

"The results concluded that..." Jessica could not believe what she was hearing. She was no longer paying attention.

"So, I would like you to come in as soon as

possible."

"Thank you," she disconnected the call. She was stunned.

For a fleeting moment, she thought of Ron, the possibility of him being in her life for years to come made her want to throw up. Wiping tears from her eyes, she realized that once again her life was about to change and she had no control over the outcome.

THANK YOU

*The story continues in...EVERYONE HAS A
SECRET*

*Please enjoy the following excerpt from
EVERYONE HAS A SECRET*

JESSICA

Everyone Has
A Secret

BOOK TWO

D. N. WATTS

1

After her conversation with her Doctor, Jessica drove directly to the beach. She parked opposite the boardwalk, shut her engine off and lowered her window, allowing the hot afternoon air into her car. She pushed her back against the seat of her car, realization setting in. She was pregnant and the scary part was, she didn't know who her baby's father was.

A flood of tears came suddenly and with such force that she could hardly breathe. Her soul felt ill, she was possibly carrying a child for a man other than her husband. For a brief moment, she considered not telling anyone that the baby might be Ron's, outside of Trey and Charmaine, no one else knew she'd slept with her ex, maybe she could convince Trey that she was pregnant with his baby. That would be a secret worth taking to her grave.

She thought that she could have the baby and she and Trey would live happily ever after. Sadly her life was no fairytale. Jessica spent the next two hours going over her options, by 5:00 p.m., she was still clueless as to what to do. She still had a few months before she actually started showing. But, she had to think of a way to tell Trey that, not only was she pregnant but that Ron might be the baby's father before too late. She grabbed a tissue from the cubby hole and dabbed at her wet eyes. Using the crumpled tissue in her hand she wiped the sweat forming on her brows while she pondered how she found herself in her current mess. She was sweating like a pig, but, she wasn't sweating solely from the humid day, her body was on fire with anxiety and stress.

Outside of the obvious, she was not sure how she felt about being pregnant just three months shy of getting married, she was not ready to be a mother, it didn't matter who the father was. She had prayed that the Plan B worked after sleeping with Ron and now she wasn't sure it did. For her, it would be better to be pregnant for her husband than her ex. There was only one option, she needed to have an abortion before she got further along in her pregnancy. She would schedule an appointment the very next day. A fresh flood of tears washed over her face as she faced a decision she never thought she would have in a million years.

Jessica felt alone and confused. She desperately wanted to talk to Charmaine, she needed confirmation that what she was about to do, was somewhat understandable under the circumstances. Her marriage would not survive this blow; she knew that Trey would leave her for good, that's something she couldn't handle again. Damn, she wouldn't even get to enjoy her honeymoon, which would have to be pushed back once more, she would need time to heal from her procedure, she didn't know what to expect after, she'd never had one before, but from what she heard from friends, the recovery can be messy and bloody.

She cleaned her face with a wet wipe and rested her head in her hands. The sun was searing through her front screen so she flipped the visor down to block the bright rays from her damp eyes. The beach looked so inviting, she wished she had a swimsuit to take a nice dip and enjoy the warm salty water. Anyway, she wasn't there to swim, groping around in her bag she found a half filled bottle of water, she took huge gulps and returned it to her bag. Her memories drifted to Ron, she was so eager to marry him and have his kids, sigh! How quickly love can turn to hate and oh boy did she hate him. There was definitely a thin line between love and hate.

She hated herself even more for being in his home alone, she remembered feeling uneasy before stepping foot inside of his condo but she shrugged it off, if only she had listened to her instincts, she would not be considering an abortion at this very moment. She wanted nothing to do with Ron and she certainly didn't want to have his baby. She took a deep breath, she had made her decision. At 6:00 p.m., she started her engine, it was time to head home; even though the sun was high, she'd stayed at the beach longer than she anticipated. Trey would be home or on his way home.

She pulled up to her curb and parked. She gathered herself and exited her car. Trey came up behind her with a barking Max. He was returning from a walk with his dog. She fluffed Max's mane and they headed inside. Trey grabbed a bottled water from the refridgerator and drank the entire thing in one swig. Jessica was trying to act normal but she was failing miserably. Trey removed Max's leash, freeing him to roam as he wished.

He sat next to her at the kitchen island.

"Are you ok?" he asked suspiciously.

She nodded yes. She felt emotionally shaken.

"Your doctor called. She wants you to pick up a prescription for your prenatal vitamins, she forgot to give you the prescription." Trey watched her reaction closely.

Jessica was sure she'd collapsed on the floor, her body felt heavy and rigid. She bitterly wished she had the ability to disappear. Barely moving her shoulders she stretched her right hand down and using her fingertips, she felt around the hard plastic of the bar chair beneath her, thankfully, she was still seated at the island and not passed out on the floor.

"Are you pregnant?" His glare felt like heated coals melting through her body. Her own saliva turned dry and was choking her at the back of her throat, she was sure dust would have puffed out of her mouth whenever she spoke.

"Jessica?" He called again.

Fucking shit. Fuck. Fuck. Fuck.

"Yes. I saw my Doctor today." She still had not made eye contact with him.

"Why didn't you call me and tell me?"

"It was a shock to me, I guess I forgot."

"Hmmm." Trey was no idiot, he knew something was up, neither did he forget that she slept with her ex a few months back.

"How far along are you?"

"I'm not sure yet." Her throat was so dry, her voice sounded croaky. She drained the few remaining droplets of water left in his bottle.

"Hmmm."

"I hate when you say that! Got damn, it's fricking annoying?" she snapped.

Trey ignored her outburst. "Is it his?" His gut wrenched and contracted as he waited for her answer.

Finally, "I don't know." She looked at him as though seeing him for the first time. His face carried no expression, she could however feel the tension building around them. A thick vein popped up in the centre of his forehead. He turned and slid out of his seat, he grabbed a cold beer from the refridgerator before kicking open the patio door. The pain and hurt hit him hard, he gulped his beer trying to fight back his own tears.

Jessica was helpless to help him in his torment, she too was stressed and she also needed comforting, she regrettably recognized that she was to blame for his upset. She pushed herself from the chair and sat next to him on the patio. She wrapped her arms around him as he sobbed uncontrollably. She wanted to tell him how sorry she was, she had said it to him so many times, she doubt it would have any effect on him.

"This is all your fault," he hissed. She was shocked and crushed by his words.

"Trey, please..."

"I'm not raising another man's baby." He was seething. "And I'm not staying in a marriage with someone who'd easily fuck her ex and stupidly get pregnant." He was practically foaming at the mouth.

Jessica felt she deserved his hate, after all she was the one who cheated. She straightened her back as her heart was pounded by the venomous words he hurled at her, his rage and fury spilling out of him; he'd never really told her how he felt about her sleeping with Ron. When he returned home from the hotel, they never discussed how he felt emotionally; in retrospect she guessed they had swept his feelings under the rug.

When Trey was finally finished ripping her a new asshole, he was very quiet.

Jessica was shocked, she was also humiliated and embarrassed. She knew that Trey loved her and she also knew her betrayal damaged a part of him. Without saying a word, she stood and went directly to her bedroom. She filled her tub to the brim, tossing in a few herbs while the hot water flowed in. She locked the bathroom door and undressed, tossing her worn clothes on the floor, she flipped her music on and perched her phone on the top shelf in the bathroom.

She eased her body into the hot water and it relaxed her immediately. Silent tears trickled down her face, Trey had never spoken to her like that before, not even in a serious argument. A choked sob echoed around her, she rolled her shoulders and flexed her neck as she tried removing the achy tension from her head and calming herself. She subconsciously rubbed her stomach.

"What am I am going to do with you now?" she smiled sheepishly.

Trey finished the last of his beer and grabbed another from the refridgerator. He returned to the patio. He was reeling from a massive headache. He was beyond pissed at Jessica. He honestly did not mean to berate her but he was sick of hearing of Ron's bitch ass. After having him taken care of by a few of his boys he was certain he was well behind them. But, she could potentially be carrying his seed. His head began throbbing painfully, he slumped onto the cold patio floor grunting against the searing pain in his head.

(End of sneak peak)

JESSICA

About The Author

Born and raised in the sunny Island of Barbados, this indie author is flexing her writing chops with her very first novel. A lover of romance and relationships, Debby-Ann has taken a unique approach to breathe life into the thoughts conceived in her fanciful mind's eye and when she is not thinking of a new tricky relationship to write about she is spending time with her family and friends